HOLLOW VENGEANCE

HOLLOW VENGEANCE

Anne Morice

St. Martin's Press
New York

Copyright © 1982 by Anne Morice
For information, write: St. Martin's Press
175 Fifth Avenue, New York, N.Y. 10010
Manufactured in the United States of America

First published in Great Britain by Macmillan London Ltd.

Library of Congress Cataloging in Publication Data

Morice, Anne.
Hollow vengeance.

I. Title.
PR6063.0743H6   1982   823'.914   81-21420
        ISBN 0-312-38834-9   AACR2

SUNDAY

One Sunday evening towards the end of last August Elsa Carrington telephoned to invite me to spend a few days, or longer if I could manage it, at her house in the country.

'I read about your play coming off,' she explained, 'and I thought you might be at a loose end.'

'How very kind of you, Elsa! I can't think of a better way of being out of work.'

This was true because, although comparatively simple and unpretentious, Elsa's house, which was called Pettits Grange and was a mile or two from the village of Sowerley, as well as her particular brand of undemanding hospitality, were such as to place her high on the list of favourite hostesses. She was quite a lot older than me, but on the other hand her two children were quite a lot younger and once or twice during the school holidays, when I was staying with my cousin Toby, who lives not far away, and when Elsa's husband was still alive, I had been roped in to babysit for them.

Admittedly, on these occasions the lines of demarcation were apt to become a little blurred once the grown-ups were safely out of the way, and an impartial observer might have found difficulty in distinguishing between the sitter and the sat with, nevertheless the awareness of being at least nominally in charge had made me feel pleasantly self-important and mature; and later on, after I had married and moved to London and it was the turn of Marcus and Emily to have school holidays, I had sometimes escorted them to Madame Tussaud's and suchlike temples of Western culture, usually followed by half a dozen courses at a Chinese restaurant.

All this had combined to make me feel as much in league with their mother's generation as with theirs and she and I had remained on good terms ever since.

5

'You had better hear the worst, before you plunge in too deep,' she now said.

'Oh, really? You mean there's a catch?'

'I wouldn't call it that exactly, but we do need all the help we can get for our campaign.'

'What campaign is that?'

'I'll give you the details when you get here, if you still decide to come, but your main job would be to join the roster.'

'Not back to babysitting again?'

'No, you could really describe this as tree-sitting.'

'That doesn't sound too arduous.'

'And, in fact, I was hoping it might suit you rather well. You could sit there quietly and learn your lines, without fear of interruption. At least, that's what we hope.'

'I haven't any lines to learn at the moment,' I admitted sadly.

'Oh, that's too bad, Tessa! Never mind, I'm sure a lovely part will turn up for you soon and, in the meantime, there's something almost as useful for you to apply yourself to, while reclining under the tree.'

'Oh, yes?'

'You can work out a way to prevent a murder.'

'How kind of you to say that, Elsa! There have been one or two hints lately that I'm better at setting them off. I shall give my all to it, to prove everyone wrong. Do tell me, though: whose murder?'

'I think that had better wait until you get here too,' she replied, so far as I could tell without a smile. 'We're in a lot of trouble here just now and one can't be too careful. Will you be driving down?'

'Yes, tomorrow afternoon, if that's okay? But don't wait tea. You can always pack mine in a basket and I'll eat it under the tree.'

Robin was watching television and when Elsa had rung off I went back to the drawing room to tell him about my strange new assignment. I had taken the call on the kitchen extension, so as not to interfere with his programme, but considered myself justified in doing so now. As a member of the Metropolitan C.I.D. he is naturally all in favour of crime prevention and I felt sure the news would come as a welcome surprise.

However, he only raised his eyebrows, warned me to take a rug, in case the grass should be damp, and went back to his American police serial.

MONDAY P.M.

Tea was in the kitchen and looked highly unappetising.

'Keep calm!' Elsa said, placing a jar of peanut butter between something called a banana cake and a large brown loaf resembling solidified porridge. 'There are some real biscuits and things, if you want them. This lot is for Millie's benefit. Fortunately, she's not often in for meals. I think it must be in your honour that she's gracing us with her company this afternoon.'

'What's all this supposed to do for her?'

'Don't ask me! Something to do with the anti-pollution programme, I understand. It's the latest fad and, if you want my opinion, I think she's got the whole thing a tiny bit wrong because she's putting on a hell of a lot of weight and I can't see how that's going to help the environmentalists very much.'

Ever since her husband's death Elsa had become increasingly bound up with her children, whom she adored, and although she often talked about them with this sort of deprecating mockery, I knew full well that anyone outside the family who dared to utter a word of criticism would be instantly felled to the ground.

'The trouble is,' she went on, 'being a strict vegetarian makes the poor child so desperately hungry that she fills up with all this stodge. "All very well fending off a heart attack," I told her, "but, if you keep this up, no attractive young man is going to care whether you get one or not".'

'Do any good?'

'Not the slightest. She's off men at the moment. I expect that's at the bottom of it, really. We reel around in a vicious circle. Oh, there you are, Millie! I was just telling Tessa about your new diet. I'm afraid you won't find a convert in her. Just look how beautifully slim she is!'

8

Emily Carrington, at this time, was a stout, somewhat pasty and inclined to be surly sixteen-year-old, who had every prospect of becoming beautiful as soon as she fined down and started preferring men to banana cake. She had inherited her mother's combination of dark hair and dark blue eyes and she had small, elegant hands and feet, which unfortunately only accentuated the clumsy obesity which, at this period, was her most striking feature.

If it was true that she had stayed at home in my honour, she must have decided that honour had now been satisfied because she glowered at me suspiciously, muttered 'hello' between clenched teeth and then ostentatiously applied herself to carving off a hunk of bread. I attributed this behaviour to self-consciousness and lack of confidence and made a mental note to take on a subsidiary task during this action-packed visit, namely to polish up her self-esteem with some liberal dollops of flattery, whenever the opportunity arose.

All the same, it was quite a relief to know that she would not be spending much time at home, because her presence had brought an awkwardness and tension into the atmosphere, not ameliorated by the fact that Elsa, doubtless with the best intentions, appeared to be going the worst way about weaning Millie off her peculiar diet, thereby creating a really heavy mother-daughter relationship, which could hardly fail to make things uncomfortable for the guest.

No reference had been made, so far, to my tree-sitting activities and I felt it might be indiscreet to mention them in front of Millie, but in fact it was she who eventually introduced the subject, although I did not immediately recognise the connection.

'Have you told Tessa about the female monster?' she asked.

'Not yet, I was waiting for you. She may as well hear the whole hideous story at one go, and I get so steamed up about it that I'd be sure to leave out the most important bits. All she knows, so far, is that she'll be doing her stint under the trees, as and when.'

'Is Marcus also concerned in this, by the way?' I asked.

'Oh, indeed! As well as a good many other people, but Marc can only do his bit at weekends. He's working terribly hard for his law exams just now. Didn't I tell you about that?'

The digression was causing Millie to become sullen and restive, so I said, 'No, but that can come later. Tell me about the monster! What's her name?'

'Mrs Trelawney. You might think that was Cornish, but no; she hails from Canada. Or rather, her last husband did. She originally came from Australia.'

'Apparently, there've been about six husbands, all told,' Millie said, 'and all stinking rich. We conclude she ate them.'

'So what's she doing here? Looking for the seventh course?'

'Shouldn't think so. She's over seventy.'

'Well, that's something on the credit side, isn't it? Perhaps she'll die a natural death quite soon? I presume she's the subject of that secondary task you've earmarked for me?' I added, turning to Elsa again. 'In which case, who's so anxious to hasten her death and why?'

'You remember Pettits Farm?' Millie asked.

'Yes, of course. In fact, wasn't this place once a part of it?'

'Till they sold it off to my grandparents about fifty years ago, but that still left six hundred acres and Mrs Trelawney now owns the lot.'

'Does she farm it?'

'Does she not!'

'That's really the crux of the matter,' Elsa explained. 'She has to farm it, of course. It's scheduled land and would be taken away from her if she didn't. Everyone understands that. It's her methods which have upset people so badly.'

'Which are?'

'More suitable for sixty thousand acres of North American corn belt. The first thing she did was to amass a huge collection of juggernaut machinery. You know, all those giant combine harvesters and things of that kind. They go thundering about, churning up the lanes and bridle paths and making no end of mess.'

'Doesn't sound like very sensible economics either.'

'No, it's not. Most of them can't manoeuvre at all in these cosy little meadows, but she's not to be beaten by that. She's had most of the hedges uprooted and now we have one forty acre field where there used to be half a dozen small ones. In a year or two we'll be living in the middle of a dust bowl.'

'But what's the point of it, Elsa? People round here have always farmed very successfully, and profitably too, if their cars and swimming pools are anything to go by. What's the point of trying to change things?'

'No point at all that anyone sane could grasp. We've all been puzzling about it for months and we've finally come to the conclusion that she suffers from a mad obsession to destroy everything in sight. She is deliberately setting out to ruin the countryside and her only pleasure seems to come from hurting people and making them unhappy.'

'Has anyone tried reasoning with her?'

'I doubt it and, in any case, it would be a practical impossibility. About the nearest you can get to her is when she's shoving you aside to get to the head of the post office queue. The only other encounters are on the roads. She drives around these lanes like a maniac, just as though they were four-lane motorways, practically forcing oncoming motorists into the ditch to avoid a collision. Apart from that, there's virtually no contact at all and she stays firmly inside her own property. It's all enclosed now in a ten foot high brick wall, with broken bottles stuck into the top of it. You know those nasty, cheap looking modern red bricks? I can't tell you how hideous and depressing it looks. And there are boards all down the length of it, saying that Trespassers Will Be Prosecuted, although who in the world would be tempted to try and get in I simply can't imagine.'

'Yes,' I admitted, 'I do begin to see that you have quite a problem here.'

'And you haven't heard the half of it,' Millie told me.

'No, she hasn't, but you take over now, Millie. I knew I should leave a lot out. It's all so horrid, I sometimes feel the only way to bear it is to put it out of my mind and pretend it isn't happening.'

'Typical of your generation!' Millie informed her grandly. 'And the main reason why odious people like Mrs Trelawney so often get away with it.'

'Although, fortunately, there can't be many people quite like her,' I remarked. 'What else has she been up to?'

'Well, she's torn down most of the old barns. They weren't all that special, so they hadn't been classified as historic buildings or anything, but they were a damn sight better than what she's put up in their place.'

'Concrete blocks with corrugated iron roofs, I suppose?'

'No, much worse. Concrete concentration camps for pigs and battery hens.'

'Yes,' Elsa said, 'I forgot to tell you that she hates animals, as well as human beings. She's ringed most of her land with electric fencing, ostensibly to keep the cattle from straying, but it wouldn't have been necessary, if she'd left the hedges alone, and it's not much fun if you want to take the dog for a walk.'

'She even tried to close all the public footpaths across her land,' Millie said, adding yet another item to the doom laden catalogue, 'but the Council stepped in at that point and told her to put her head in a bucket. So how do you think she got round that one?'

'Can't imagine!'

'By putting up notices on all the stiles, saying Beware of the Bull.'

'My God!'

'I know, it's absolutely revolting, isn't it? She's only got two bulls and obviously they can't be in forty places at once, but not many people feel like risking it on their afternoon walk. Whatever we do, she somehow manages to go one better. We've no sooner formed a rescue squad to go prowling around at night, cutting the electric wires and knocking down the notice boards, than she dreams up some new hellish idea. Trees are coming in for the treatment now. Anything which stands in the path of the plough gets the chop and she's cutting them down like nettles.'

'But listen, Millie, surely the Council can get her there too? I always understood that you had to get permission to cut down trees, even those on your own land?'

'That's the law, in theory,' Elsa explained, 'but there are dozens of ways for unprincipled people to get round it, if they have a mind to. You can say that they've got Dutch Elm disease, or are quietly and invisibly rotting away inside and constitute a danger to the public. In other words, you act first and talk later and, if anyone complains, the worst that can happen to you is to be fined about fifty pounds, which would mean less than nothing to someone like Mrs Trelawney.'

'So now you're having to mount guard round all the trees? Sounds like a pretty formidable undertaking?'

'Oh yes, and far too ambitious for a group like ours to cope with, but there's one in particular which we know to be on the execution list and for the moment we're concentrating on that. It's in a hollow and the land is quite unworkable, so she has no excuse at all and it also happens to be a very special local landmark. It's a magnificent oak and about two hundred years old, so they say. We mean to protect it, if we can, partly to show her that we're not beaten yet, but mainly because of what it would do to poor old Geoffrey to lose his beloved tree.'

'Geoffrey? You mean that nice, old-maidish little man who offers one wine gums and writes those whimsy little pamphlets about the local beauty spots? *Strolls Through Storhampton* and so forth? Geoffrey Darling, or some name like that?'

'Dearing. Yes, he's the one.'

'And you're telling me this philistine has designs on his cherished oak?'

'The trouble is that, technically, it's not really his at all. It's on the wrong side of the fence; but only a few yards inside the boundary and, naturally, after all these years, he feels a sense of ownership and dedicated duty to protect it.'

'Because, you see,' Millie added, 'when he's not munching wine gums and writing his whimsy pamphlets, he's sitting in front of the window, munching wine gums and gazing with dazzled eyes at the beautiful oak.'

'Understandable,' I admitted. 'I remember it well and I could so easily find myself similarly occupied, if I could see it from my window.'

'So far, we've managed to head her off,' Elso said. 'Twice now, the men have rolled up with their ladders and chain saws and either Geoffrey or someone else has been there to shoo them away again. We hope to wear her down with our eternal vigilance.'

'But what bribery or persuasion did you use on them? Apart, that is, from crying: "Woodman, spare this tree!"?'

'Passive resistance!' Millie replied, with a crusading light in her eye.

'Oh, I see! You literally flatten yourself against the trunk and instruct them to proceed over your dead body?'

'Fortunately, it hasn't come to that yet,' Elsa said, 'and let's hope it won't. The poor men would be most embarrassed. We just tell them that there's an injunction on it, or some nonsense and that they might be in trouble with the law. On the whole, they're quite relieved just to slink away. Obviously, they never had much heart for the business in the first place. Which reminds me, Millie: who's on guard this afternoon?'

'Oh, Geoffrey's there and on the watch. I promised to be there by about six and stay till it gets dark. He's going to drinks with the Ramseys.'

'Then you'd better get your skates on, because it's nearly six now.'

'Okay,' she replied, getting up and hacking off a large slice of banana cake, which she wrapped in a paper napkin and stuffed in her pocket, before leaving the room.

Watching her go, Elsa sighed: 'Problems, problems! The

14

place is stiff with them just now. And I haven't even begun to tell you about Marcus yet. I think I'd better wait until we've both got a drink in our hands before I embark on that.'

I was not, after all, to hear about Marcus's problem until much later, because by the time we both had a drink in our hands Elsa had started to get worked up about the dinner. She had invited my cousin Toby, under the impression, for some reason, that I would be burning to see him, and he had accepted.

I was faintly surprised to hear this, because he does not much care for dining in other people's houses and normally has a whole battery of excuses to hand, when faced with such emergencies. I think Elsa had been rather taken aback too, but she discovered later that Mr and Mrs Parkes were on holiday, which explained everything. Mr Parkes looks after Toby's garden and his wife rules the domestic roost, a job which she has performed with the utmost efficiency and ironest of rods for many years. I seriously doubt whether Toby could any longer find his way to his own kitchen.

Elsa's cooking was not up to the Parkes standard, but luckily Millie was engaged elsewhere for the evening, so at least she had no need to divert part of her energies into boiling up great mounds of brown rice, which she informed me would otherwise have been the case.

'Where's she gone?' I enquired. 'And, if she's off boys, how does she come to have such a busy social programme?'

'Oh, she and a few friends of like persuasion have dis-covered a macrobiotic restaurant in Dedley and they go drifting off there once or twice a week, usually ending up in the cinema. I believe some of them actually are boys, as a matter of fact, but you can hardly tell, so I don't suppose they count.'

'That's all right, then. I was afraid Toby might have scared her off.'

'Oh no, he wouldn't count either. Far too old.'

Nevertheless, and despite this built-in advantage, it was

15

just as well, from several points of view, that she was not with us. He would inevitably have blotted his copybook, or perhaps merely confirmed her in the view that senility was another word for the mid-forties, by his scathing dismissal of the anti-Trelawney campaign.

'Absolute madness!' he informed Elsa. 'It never does to oppose people of that sort when they hold all the cards. You'll only wear yourself out by trying to descend to her level and, being an amateur at that game, you still won't win. In fact, by fighting her you are probably simply adding fuel to her flames.'

'I don't know where we should all be now, if everyone had taken that attitude,' she protested mildly.

'Exactly where we are, I daresay. Sensible people have always known where the better part of valour lay. The time for killing dragons is when you're encased in a heavy suit of armour and equipped with a long, sharp sword.'

'And what do you do when you have neither? Sit back and wait for the dragon to come and eat you up?'

'No, you move to a place where all the dragons have been killed off already, or have yet to be born. It need not be very far away. If you really want my advice, you'll sell this house, preferably tomorrow or the day after, before the word gets round about what is going on here and the bottom drops out of the market.'

'Yes,' Elsa agreed reluctantly, 'I daresay you have a point there. It would probably be the most practical solution, but unfortunately it is not open to me. Not if I wish to remain on speaking terms with Marcus and Millie.'

Toby did not comment and she added defensively, 'I can tell from your expression that you would regard that as a small price to pay, but it would be a huge one for me. They're all I have, you know, and they're both mad about this place.'

'Yes, but the point is, Elsa dear, that you're not going to have them for ever, are you? At least, not quite in the same way. In a few years from now they'll be off creating a different sort of hell for someone else and you'll be left sitting all alone in your dust bowl.'

'I hope not, Toby. In fact, I rather expect it to be the other way round. This place belonged to my family, you know, not my husband's. My parents moved out when I married and I hope to do the same one day for Marc or Millie. Besides, that's not the whole story, or even half of it. They're like all their generation, absolutely potty about ecology and conservation and so on. They regard Mrs Trelawney as the enemy, but also as a challenge, and they'd never forgive me if I surrendered in the first round.'

'Better than being knocked out cold in the tenth, I should have thought,' Toby said, 'but I can see that nothing I could say would do anything to change your mind and . . . strangely enough, I'm rather glad, in a way.'

Elsa and I being somewhat thunderstruck by this swift reversal, he was kind enough to explain.

'It has given me an idea for a play. I am not sure how it will end, or even begin, for that matter, but naturally I shall be following your progress with some interest.'

'According to Elsa, if we don't look out, it will end with the old harridan getting herself murdered,' I told him.

'Oh no, I don't care for that at all. I shall be looking for something much less crude and obvious.'

'So shall I!' Elsa agreed fervently.

'Then obviously you and Toby should pool your resources. He will find a nice, neat theatrical ending and you must somehow translate it into real life.'

'So at least one good thing has come out of this,' I remarked an hour or two later, when Toby had gone home and we were loading up the dishwasher.

'Indeed? Do tell me!'

'Toby's idea for a play. You know how hard it is for him to put pen to paper and how he suffers from this dread of going to the grave without ever finding the urge to write another line? If you've really managed to shake him out of it, however briefly, it must do some good.'

17

'You don't think he was serious?'

'Something tells me he was, although time alone will tell. Are you too tired to tell me about Marc now?'

'Yes, I think it had better wait until the morning. Millie might come in at any moment. There is a very strict and well understood rule that she has to be home by eleven, and just occasionally she has been known to observe it.'

'And this is not for her ears?'

'Strictly speaking, not for anyone's. Entirely my own fault for not warning you, but for a moment I was terrified you were going to blow the gaff to Toby.'

'How could I have blown it when I didn't know what the gaff was?'

'It was when you told him that this could end with Mrs Trelawney getting herself murdered.'

'Well?'

'Well, that's the worry, you see. Marc's the one who's been going around making these silly threats that, if no other solution can be found, he, personally, will undertake to devise and carry out the perfect murder.'

'You do see how very awkwardly it could turn out?' she said about twenty minutes later, I having stubbornly refused to go to bed until I had heard every detail of Marc's eccentric plan.

Fortunately, this had been one of those rare occasions when Millie had obeyed the strict and well understood rule and, after taking a pained look at the remains of the sirloin, which still adorned the kitchen table, had gone straight up to her room.

So we finished the clearing away and then sat in the kitchen, drinking warmed up coffee and waiting for the dishwasher to go through its paces, while she gave me the full story.

'I mean, just think of it, Tessa! Suppose the old woman were to drop dead from a stroke or something? And it could easily happen, you know! She's over seventy and they say she flies into the most terrible rages when she can't get her own way. Well, if something of that sort did happen and people were to remember Marc's ridiculous threats, you can imagine all the talk there'd be? Not malicious, necessarily, although I daresay there'd be a bit of that too. He's not the most popular boy in the neighbourhood and you know how people fasten on to gossip in a small place like this?'

I was tempted to ask why he was not the most popular boy in the neighbourhood, since, as well as being good looking, he had always impressed me as possessing plenty of charm. However, in view of the lateness of the hour, I considered it advisable to stick to essentials and I said, 'But it's all rather absurd, surely? They couldn't seriously believe that he had murdered her and, even if they did, they would very quickly be proved wrong.'

'I know, but imagine all the unpleasantness we should have to endure in the meantime! And afterwards there would probably still be some people muttering that there was no smoke without fire; because I'm afraid that the forces of law and order would be obliged to treat it seriously, whether they wished to or not.'

'Why would they?'

'Because Marc has a very special motive, all of his own. He is in love, well, engaged perhaps I should say, to a girl whose family is about to be evicted from their home by Mrs You-Know-Who.'

'The final touch of melodrama! It was the only thing lacking. Who is she?'

'A girl called Diane Hearne. You probably wouldn't know her. James, the father, makes pottery, some of it rather good too, but he's not, by any stretch of the imagination, what you'd call successful; and the mother's delicate and mentally unstable. She's had to bring up five children on practically no money, no help and no mod cons, so I suppose she has every excuse.'

'Where do they live?'

'Orchard House, which is on the Pettits estate, and there's the rub. The Hearnes rented it from the previous owners about twenty years ago, when it was falling to pieces from neglect. It's not in much better shape now, but they've done their best to make a few improvements and keep it in reasonably good trim. In return for which they've been paying just a tiny peppercorn rent.'

'Even so, didn't they have a lease?'

'Yes, which was renewed annually, it now appears. The Hearnes are like that, completely hand-to-mouth and feckless, and James is the worst of the lot. When they heard that the property had been acquired by a solitary old lady, it never occurred to them that things wouldn't run on in exactly the same way as before. They were prepared for their rent to go up, naturally, but with Diane out of school now and in a job of sorts, that wouldn't have been such a terrible blow. Instead, they got a notice to quit as soon as the present lease expires and not a single day later. That was three or four months ago and I imagine their time is now rapidly running out.'

'So what will they do?'

'So far, they don't appear to be doing anything. Mrs Hearne had quite a serious breakdown and had to go into hospital for a while; James, who is a real Micawber type, seems to take the view that something is bound to turn up to save the day, while Marc goes around loudly threatening to take matters into his own hands; and that seems to be about the sum of it.'

'Can't they appeal? How about possession being nine-tenths of the law?'

'My dear Tessa, you obviously still haven't understood what we're up against. The woman doesn't miss a single trick and, as Toby pointed out, she also holds all the cards. You or I couldn't turn the Hearnes out of a house they'd been living in for twenty years, but Mrs Trelawney only has to say that she needs it for her workers and there's no further argument.'

'Which could be genuine, I suppose? All those fancy bits of machinery must need a lot of extra men?'

'On the contrary. If you knew the first thing about farming, you'd realise that they cut down on manpower, which is something else that hasn't made her very popular with the natives; but what she has the effrontery to say is that she needs this particular house, out of half a dozen others which one would have thought equally suitable, for her estate manager, who also happens to be her grandson.'

'Ah! I'd been meaning to ask whether she'd acquired any family from her various marriages?'

'He's the only one, so far as we know. She had a son early on in her career, but she quarrelled with him over his choice of wife, or so we hear, and he went back to Australia and took up sheep farming.'

'In the time honoured style?'

'Although, of course, that's where the roots were, in his case. Still, you're right, the whole dreary saga is not unlike some Victorian melodrama. Even down to David, the hand-some young grandson she's never seen, coming back in the other direction to seek his fame and fortune over here. He ought to be the hero of the piece, but no one feels too con-fident about that.'

'Not the second villain, I trust?'

'It wouldn't altogether surprise me. It didn't take him long to discover where his fame and fortune lay, to change his name by deed poll to hers and to instal himself as the young laird. Quite what qualifications he has for a job of this kind no one really knows, but he certainly has his old grannie eating out of his hand, by all accounts.'

'That's interesting too,' I said.

'You think so?'

'Yes, because if you're going to put a spoke in her wheel, or her Achilles heel, you'll need to find out where she's most vulnerable. This David could be the answer. What's he like, apart from being good looking and having an eye to the main chance?'

'Pleasant enough, actually, and certainly more socially engaging than his grandmother. Quite good manners and all that, but there's something about him that I don't entirely trust. Let's go to bed now, shall we? I'm all in.'

'Me too,' I agreed, putting away the last plate, although, as it happened, the night had not finished with us yet. We were scarcely half way upstairs when there were three loud knocks on the front door, causing me to clutch the bannister rail in alarm, although Elsa seemed more annoyed than apprehensive.

'Who the hell could that be?' she asked.

Since I was in no position to tell her, I did not reply and, being unaccustomed to casual country ways, watched in amazement as she unlocked the front door, opened it a few inches and called out:

'Who is it? Who's there?'

I could hear a man's voice answering, though the words were too indistinct to make out, but Elsa unhesitatingly pulled the door wide open, saying, 'Why, Tim! Whatever's the matter? Is something wrong?'

I went slowly downstairs again and this time I could hear him plainly.

'Very sorry to bother you, Elsa, but I saw your lights on and I wondered if I might ask you for a bowl of water?'

At this point, possibly wandering a little in the mists of fatigue, I began to think I must have slipped into one of those old fashioned Westerns and that a lady passenger on the stage coach was about to give birth, but Elsa's reaction was more prosaic.

'Yes, of course. Is your engine boiling, or something? Do come inside!'

Doing so, he said, 'No, it's for Daisy, our retriever. Poor old girl's been caught in one of those beastly snares. Probably been lying out there for hours.'

'Oh, my dear Tim, how dreadful for you! Is she badly hurt?'

'Can't say, until I get her down to the vet in the morning, but it looks as though one front leg is a goner. She's pretty exhausted too and thirsty, I imagine, so I ventured to knock you up, late though it is.'

'Let me fetch it?' I suggested.

'No, no, Tessa, you don't know where anything is. You stay here. I won't be a moment, Tim.'

He was a thin, pale, twisted up sort of man, with gold rimmed glasses and a disdainful manner. I judged him to be forty, or a little over, and he was somewhat eccentrically dressed in á formal suit, with the trousers tucked into heavy black rubber boots. He was also afflicted by a nervous tic, or, to be accurate, two. The most constant and noticeable affected his facial muscles, jerking down the corners of his mouth in a spasm which at times became so pronounced that it spread to his whole face and produced an involuntary sneering grimace of anger and disgust. The other, milder and less frequent, was of brushing the palm of his right hand with a folded handkerchief, but in a perfunctory way, as though the urge to remove the damn'd spot had turned from a driving compulsion into a fixed habit.

'How d'you do? My name's Macadam,' he announced, in a clipped, staccato voice, as though the words were being forced out of him against his will.

'And I'm Theresa Crichton.'

I was chagrined to notice that he did not appear to be particularly thrilled to hear it, but of course he had more pressing matters on his mind and, furthermore, if this kind of misadventure befell him often, he obviously did not get much opportunity to watch television.

'You were lucky to find her, weren't you?' I suggested. 'In the dark and everything?'

'I wouldn't say luck had much to do with it,' he replied snappishly. 'She's been missing since lunch time. When I got back from my office this evening there was a note from my wife, telling me which areas she was covering and which I should take on. I just pulled on some boots and off I went. Even so, I was tramping around the woods for three or four hours before I happened to hear poor old Daisy whimpering.'

'What sort of animal was the snare intended for?'

'Foxes, presumably.'

23

'Isn't it awfully cruel?'

'Awfully irresponsible, which is slightly more to the point. Not that the lady in question would give a damn about that, or care whose dog happened . . . Oh, thank you so much,' he said, losing interest in me, as Elsa returned, carrying a large pudding basin.

'Don't bother to bring it back,' she told him. 'Just leave it by the gate and I'll pick it up in the morning. That is, if you're sure there's nothing else I can do?'

'Well, if you'd be so good as to give Louise a ring? Tell her what's happened and that I'm on my way. If I know her, she won't sleep a wink until she knows that Daisy is safe.'

'Yes, of course, I'll see to it right away.'

'Oh, and tell her not to worry if I'm not back for half an hour or so. I'll have to take it dead slow, to try and avoid any jolts.'

'Yes, right you are, Tim, and good luck! I do hope it won't turn out to be serious.'

'More of Mrs Trelawney's work, do you suppose?' I asked, as she picked up the telephone.

'Oh, undoubtedly. Charming, isn't it? You begin to see why we all feel so persecuted? We soon shan't dare to go near the woods, for fear of getting mangled in a gin trap, or falling into an elephant hole.'

'That's odd!' she said a moment or two later. 'No reply.'

'Are you trying the right number?'

'At this time of night I couldn't be certain of anything. Be a dear and check it for me in that address book. Under Macadam.'

'Tim and Louise? Two-one-three-eight.'

'Right! One more try and then we'll give up and go to bed.'

'So perhaps he doesn't know her quite so well as he thinks?' I suggested, when she had dialled the number again and waited for over a minute.

'It's odd though, don't you think? Even if she had been asleep, surely the telephone would have woken her by now?'

'Unless she's still out, searching for the dog herself?'

'Oh, hardly, Tessa! It's past midnight.'

'All the same, I had the impression they were both Daisy fanatics a bit above the norm.'

'Well, I admit they are inclined to treat the creature as though it were human, but that's only because their only child was killed in a road accident a year or two ago and they've had to find something to fill her place. But Louise is not the hysterical type at all; very clear-headed and practical, in fact. Never mind, there's nothing we can do about it and we really should go to bed, you know. Don't forget your tree watching starts tomorrow.'

'Yes, that's right. What time does Geoffrey want me there?'

'Rather early, I'm afraid. Everything in Geoffrey's life is organised down to the last wine gum and he likes to get all his household supplies in for the whole week on Tuesday morning, as soon as the shops open. No use expecting Millie to be conscious at that hour, so I'll give you a shout about seven.'

I was not entirely confident about my own chances of being conscious at that hour and made a mental note to take a pillow with me, as well as the rug, in the hope of catching a quick snooze under the tree.

TUESDAY A.M.

When the time came, however, neither pillow nor rug was needed. We were on the point of leaving the house, in the cool dawn of Tuesday morning, when the telephone rang. Millie was still in bed, so Elsa had to go indoors again to answer it. Being compulsively interested in other people's lives, or as some would say, inquisitive, I followed her, being eager to learn who had something so urgent to convey that it could not wait for a more godly hour.

Urgent it undoubtedly was and distressing as well. That much I could tell from Elsa's expression; from her words only that the caller was Louise, with a long, long tale to unfold. The one-sided conversation lasted for seven or eight minutes.

At the end of it Elsa replaced the receiver with a trembling hand and regarded me in silence for a moment or two, as though formulating the words to announce that this country was now at war.

What she in fact said was, 'That was Louise Macadam.'

'I gathered. About the dog?'

'Oh no, no. She gave up that search as soon as it started to get dark, but when she got home and was drawing the curtains she saw some lights down in the hollow between their house and Geoffrey's cottage. They looked like head-lights, three or four pairs of them in a semi-circle. She guessed immediately what it meant and she went straight downstairs again, got her bicycle out and rode down there. There were no lights on in the cottage and no answer when she rang the bell, so she went round to the back. There wasn't a sound and the lights had gone too, but she was just able to see the outline of the tree and for a moment she thought she'd gone mad, because it had completely changed.'

Elsa had recited all this in a completely flat and

26

expressionless tone, which did not reflect her feelings, for her eyes were now filled with tears.

'Oh, goodness, Elsa, how simply terrible! And I suppose the poor woman had to wait there for Geoffrey to come home, so that she could warn him?'

'No, worse than that, much worse! He'd come home already, before she arrived. Obviously, the cars and lights had still been there at that point, for he must have started running down towards the fence. Louise found him when she went towards it herself, to get a closer look at the tree. He was lying on the ground, unconscious.'

'Not dead, though?'

'She wasn't absolutely sure, but she thought he was still breathing. It was difficult to make out what had happened to him, or what state he was in, because it was almost completely dark by then. She nearly went out of her mind, wondering what to do and how to get help.'

'So what did she do?'

'Went back to the cottage, but, as she'd forseen, both doors were locked and the downstairs windows tightly shut. He can't have gone indoors at all. They're leaded casement windows and the only tool she had was her bicycle pump, but she managed to break a pane of glass with that and release the catch, so that she could climb inside.'

'Very resourceful!'

'Yes, as I told you, in most ways she's got her head well screwed on. Which reminds me! How awful of me! I quite forgot to ask her about Daisy,' Elsa added, as though this was the last straw.

'Well, never mind about that now. Go on about Geoffrey!'

'Not much more to tell. After she'd climbed in, she telephoned for an ambulance and waited outside until it came, which she said seemed like hours, but was probably not more than about twenty minutes. She went with him to the hospital and waited there for what really was hours, until the specialist had seen him.'

'And?'

'A major heart attack. They'd put him into intensive care and Louise got the impression that his chances of ever coming out again are fairly remote. When she rang the hospital about half an hour ago, they told her he was comfortable, but that his condition was unchanged, so presumably he could be most uncomfortable, for all they know.'

'So now it's just watch and pray?'

'No, there are a few practical jobs to be seen to, as it happens. Louise has to get hold of someone to mend the broken window, for a start. She managed to persuade the hospital authorities to hand over the front door key, which was still in his pocket and she wants me to meet her there this morning and help her go through some of his papers. The purpose of that is to try and discover who his solicitor is, in case there are any relatives who ought to be informed. That's the kind of thing that probably wouldn't have occurred to me in a million years, but it's typical of Louise. As I told you, she's blazingly practical in most ways.'

'Yes, so you did,' I agreed thoughtfully, although my thoughts were not really on Louise. I was wondering how this new turn of events might be incorporated into Toby's play, for it seemed to me that what we had here was quite a good twist on which to bring the curtain down on Act One, Scene One. Everyone in Elsa's circle appeared to be hoping, or perhaps in her case dreading, to hear that Mrs Trelawney had dropped dead, but now it looked as though she had been cast as murderer, instead of victim. If Geoffrey were not to recover from his heart attack, there could be no denying that, morally speaking, it would be she who had killed him.

No one subscribed to this view more vehemently than Millie and, before leaving to meet Louise, Elsa warned me what to expect.

'I had to tell her the whole brutal truth,' she explained. 'Short of bundling her on to the afternoon train to Bristol, there was simply no possibility of keeping it from her.'

'How did she take it?'

'Badly. Very badly, in fact. I try to console myself by remembering how much more quickly one gets over these things at her age, but of course we have to face the fact that there may be worse to come with Geoffrey, and that's the part which upsets her most. She really dotes on the old boy.'

'In spite of his being a man?'

'Well, only in the technical sense. In some ways, he's more like an elderly child. She feels protective about him and now, of course, she's howling about bringing a lawsuit against Mrs Trelawney and getting her shut up in an asylum for the criminally insane.'

'Might not be such a bad idea.'

'Only rather difficult to put into practice. And we'll have to go through the whole thing again with Marc on Friday. It hardly bears thinking about. I know this hasn't been much fun for you, so far, Tessa, but I do hope you'll stay and see me through the weekend?'

'Certainly, if I can be of any use.'

'The greatest possible. They both like you so much and you help to bridge the generation gap.'

It was agreed that I should stay at least until Monday and also that when Robin telephoned that evening I should invite him for the weekend.

Millie came downstairs about an hour later and it was evident that she had been crying, which was not something she was advised to indulge in often. Her slanting, blue-grey eyes, which were her most attractive feature, had almost disappeared inside her head.

Elsa had left out a dish of raw carrots and the rocklike loaf, but Millie had no appetite for them and announced in a hoarse voice that she was going for a walk. I suspected that the object was to pile Pelion on Ossa by making a personal inspection of the mutilated tree. Perhaps there was an element of masochism in this, but nevertheless I considered that she was probably wise to get the worst impact over as quickly as possible and I said that, if she had no objection, I would accompany her.

She did not, as I had anticipated, set off to the right in the direction of the valley and Geoffrey's cottage, but led the way in the opposite direction, along an upward path through the woods.

'Where are we going?' I asked her.

'Just along here for about half a mile. It comes out on the ridge and you can see right down over the valley.'

'Yes, I remember. We used to have picnics there when you and Marc were tots.'

'Still do.'

'And you can see the oak tree from there, as I remember?'

'Sort of aeroplane view of it. I want to get some idea of how bad it is before I . . .'

'Zoom in for the close-up?'

'Right!'

'Listen, Millie, I know this sounds stuffy and patronising, but it's not the end of the world, whatever you may think now. And I daresay even Mrs Trelawney will relent, or be scared into calling off the operation, when she hears about the havoc it's caused. Then the tree will get back to its original glory eventually and Geoffrey may recover too.'

'I'm not sure that I want him to. His life would be quite spoilt now.'

'Oh, people are much more resilient than that. I do realise how shocking it will be for him initially, but there are other things in life besides trees, you know.'

'But it isn't only the tree, Tessa, it's what it represents. It's sort of like a permanent threat. None of the things we've always taken for granted seem to be safe any more.'

We were approaching the full sunlight at the edge of the wood by this time and she darted ahead on her own, as though anxious for the climax to be a solitary experience, going at a fair clip, too, considering her weight, and I did not attempt to keep pace with her.

When I caught up she was sitting on the grass, staring out over the open landscape, and hunger had evidently caught up with her too, because she was absent-mindedly pulling some rather wizened looking blackberries off a nearby bush and stuffing them into her mouth.

'No use, is it?' she asked, without turning her head, as I plopped down beside her. 'You don't get any particular impression from here. I'll have to see it on the same level to take it in properly. Would you come with me this afternoon? Ma and Louise ought to be through at the cottage by then. I couldn't stand having them around, wringing their hands and worrying about whether I was going into hysterics or something. But I'd like to have you there, to give some moral support.'

Touched to the quick, I said, 'Sure! And, what's more, I've had an idea. Let's take a camera with us.'

'What for? I shan't need reminders or souvenirs, if that's what you're thinking.'

'No, it isn't. What I'm thinking is something quite different. Which day does *The Dedley Mercury* come out?'

'Friday.'

'And today's only Tuesday. That's fine! I've brought one of those polaroid, instant things with me, so I should think we can just make it. And you can write the copy. Your mother tells me you plan to take a course in journalism when you leave school, so it'll be good practice for you.'

'What are you on about, Tessa?'

'Publicity. It's one of the most effective weapons there is in the civil disobedience game and I've picked up a few tips in my time. So here's what we'll do. We'll go home now and ring up the editor of *The Mercury* and make an appointment with him, preferably for tomorrow morning.'

'What makes you think he'll buy it?'

'I expect he will. It's worth a try, anyway. He may just conceivably have seen my name on the credits, which might help to oil the wheels, but if necessary we can probably manage without that.'

'What do we say then?'

'That there's been a serious outbreak of vandalism around here, which is bringing the local community to its knees and,

31

furthermore, that we can produce photographs to illustrate one of the worst outrages. Incidentally, it might be worth getting one of Daisy, dangling her wounded paw and looking very forlorn and lovable.'

'But won't the old woman sue us for libel, or something?'

'No, because we'll stick firmly to facts, all of which can be proved. And, naturally, no names will be mentioned, simply a well placed hint or two that this is not the work of mindless hooligans, but a carefully planned campaign on the part of a powerful minority to destroy the environment. We shall also say that we have witnesses by the dozen to back us up and that an editorial on the subject in his fearless, hard-hitting, uncompromising journal will send the circulation figures whizzing up and keep the presses humming far into the night.'

'Not half bad, Tessa! Better than sitting around and moping, anyway, and a million times better than that stupid brother of mine stamping about and threatening to commit murder, if he has to. Come on, let's go home and get started on it!'

'I'm really puzzled by Marc,' I remarked as we tramped along. 'You'd think a law student, of all people, would be a bit more discreet.'

'You would, wouldn't you? But it's only the sort of wild, showing off joke he goes in for sometimes. At least, I hope that's all it is. We agreed ages ago that non-violence was the only civilised answer to aggression, but of course that was before he got into the clutches of Diane.'

'You think she may have influenced him in the other direction?'

'Wouldn't put it past her.'

'Well, I haven't met her, as you know, but she didn't sound a particularly violent type from your mother's description.'

'Maybe not, but she's a whiner and probably the kind who incites other people to violence, which is even more despicable. Actually, I think she's either a complete fake or a bit mad.'

'Really? In what way?'

'When I said she was a whiner, I should have chosen my words more carefully because she never actually complains about anything. She's more like – martyred, if you know what I mean? Always so sweet and patient and putting a brave face on everything. It's enough to make you sick sometimes.'

'Because you think it's an act?'

'Yes, I do; and not a half bad one, either. Everyone says she's such a saint and they dash about doing everything they can to help her, while she just sits back and says how frightfully kind they are and never actually moves a muscle to help herself.'

'Has she always been like that? I assume you've known each other since you were children?'

'Oh, you bet! And she was always being held up to the rest of us as such a blasted model. I'll tell you the kind of thing she used to do, Tessa. Some stupid kid at a party would burst its balloon and start howling and we'd all say Oh, bad luck! or Shut up! or something, but Diane would dash up and coo: "Oh, please don't cry, darling, have mine! Oh, go on, you must, I don't mind a bit!" Then all the mothers would say what a poppet she was and they'd give her two balloons as a reward. That was when she was about eight and she hasn't changed one bit.'

Millie's voice had taken on a most nauseating simper while she was imitating Diane, and I said, 'I rather hope I don't have to meet her.'

'Fraid you're bound to, if you're going to be here for the weekend. She'll be round in a flash as soon as Marc arrives, gazing into his eyes and telling him how wonderful he is!'

'I can see that he would find that rather intoxicating, specially after being bullied by you for most of his life.'

'Well, I find it revolting and I think Ma does too, although nothing would induce her to admit it. Diane never stops jumping about and asking what she can do to help and saying how tired Ma looks and what a shame she doesn't have anyone to help her, which is a side swipe at me, of course; and also treating her as though she was practically senile, which you can see getting on her nerves. And the end of it is that Diane never actually lifts a finger, although no one except me seems to notice that. I could really throttle her sometimes.'

I refrained from pointing out that it might be difficult to square this with the policy of non-violence and we spent the remaining few minutes of the walk discussing plans for our attack on the editor of *The Dedley Mercury*.

They could not be translated into action as speedily as we would have wished, though, because when we arrived back at the Grange Elsa had not returned, but we had a visitor. She was one of the prettiest girls I had ever seen, aged about nineteen or twenty and whose only flaw was in having teeth which were too small and babyish, showing far too much gum whenever she smiled, and smiling was something she went in for in rather a big way.

She was dowdily dressed in a limp looking, flowered cotton skirt and brown, handknitted cardigan. Whether this was because she lacked both money and taste I could not tell, but curiously enough it hardly detracted at all from her flaxen beauty, which was of that rare variety which needed no embellishment whatever. Whereas her personality would probably have been just as irritating if she had been got up like the star of a television spectacular and hung about with emeralds and pearls.

She was seated like Patience on a Sofa, with hands folded demurely on her lap and a sweet, sad expression on her face, but jumped up when we came into the room, the hands now outstretched and tears brimming in the huge violet-blue eyes. Her intention was evidently to embrace Millie, but it was one of those instances of she who kisses and she who turns the cheek, and Millie turned hers so fast that the kiss missed its target by inches.

'What are you doing here?' she asked, so aggressively as to dispel any remaining doubts about the identity of the visitor, who replied in a breathless, little-girl voice:

34

'Oh, please don't be cross with me for walking in like this, but the door was open, so I thought you might be back soon and I'm so dreadfully worried by all these rumours we've been hearing about poor old Mr Dearing. Do tell me, is it really true that he. . . ?'

'Yes, it is, but why aren't you at work? Have you got the sack or something?'

'Oh no, although I'm afraid it may come to that, if I have to stay away too long. I can't help it though. This is one of those times when I simply have to put poor Mummy first.'

'Why? Is she ill again? This is Tessa Price, by the way, also known as Theresa Crichton. Tessa, allow me to present Diane Hearne.'

'Oh, how do you do, Mrs Price? How simply super to meet you! Goodness, what an unexpected thrill! No, not ill exactly, Millie, just a wee bit run down and depressed. Daddy and I both think that what she needs is a little holiday, so I've told them I shan't be coming in to the office for a few days and tomorrow morning I'm going to take her down to stay with her sister in Bexhill. It's only a tiny bungalow, but we'll manage somehow and I shan't mind a bit sleeping on the floor,' Diane informed us, modestly lowering her eyes, as though to acknowledge our applause, which in fact was silent.

'Does my brother know you're going?'

'No, not yet. It was all fixed up in such a hurry. I've written a tiny note for him, though, and I wondered if you'd be an angel and put it in his room for me?'

'Okay, but why not ring him up and explain? Why leave it till he gets here to find out?'

Diane, looking pained, did not reply and Millie waited.

'Well, if you must know, Millie. . . . Well, I expect it's hard for you to understand, because you've never been in this situation, I'm thankful to say, but things are rather difficult at home just now. Money problems, among other things, and I'm trying to be most fearfully careful and not use the telephone unless it's for something absolutely vital. Sorry to be

35

such a bore about all these family troubles,' she added, turning to me, with a rueful smile this time, 'I'd so much rather talk about you, and your wonderful glamorous life, but Millie never gives one any peace until she's dragged out all the shameful secrets.'

'I am not bored in the least,' I assured her, 'never less so.'

If the object had been to shame Millie into silence for her lack of sensitivity, it could not be said to have succeeded, because she said, 'Then why not use our telephone? Go on, call him up now! Ma won't mind a bit.'

'Oh no, I couldn't possibly,' Diane said hurriedly and speaking, it seemed to me, spontaneously for the first time.

'Why not? You can use the upstairs extension, if you don't want us to hear.'

'It's not that, but ... well, I mean, he'll be working now, won't he?'

'Only slogging away at home for the exam, all alone in his mean little bedsitter. He'll be thrilled if you interrupt him.'

'No, Millie dear, thank you very much, but I'd rather not. I know you mean to be kind, but I'm so awfully stupid at explaining things on the telephone and I've put it all in my note. Besides, Mummy needs me at home, to help her pack. She gets into a frightful flap if I'm not there to tell her what she'll need, poor darling. So thanks again, but I really must dash now.'

And dash she did, out of the room and out of the house, as one pursued by a bear.

'Something fishy there,' Millie remarked when she had gone.

'I agree.'

'Honestly, Tessa? Gosh that makes me feel better!'

She looked better too. The flush of pleasure, added now to the light of battle in her eye, did marvels for her complexion and the sullen droop of her mouth had temporarily disappeared. It was gratifying, but at the same time slightly baffling that one simple observation could have brought about such a transformation.

Millie explained: 'You see, I had really begun to be afraid that I was getting obsessions about her and that, underneath, I'm just plain old jealous, because she's so beautiful and has such a wonderful figure and everyone thinks she's such an unselfish little dream boat. All the things, in fact which I'm not.'

'Oh, I wouldn't call her beautiful,' I said.

'Good for you! That's nice to hear too, but most people do, you know.'

'She's pretty, I admit, but it's not the kind that lasts. She'll be quite ordinary looking in another fifteen or twenty years, whereas you'll always be all right because you've got good bones.'

I felt rather daring in saying this, because the sad truth was that, now that Millie was padded out with so much excess weight, it was impossible to tell whether her bones were good or bad, or indeed whether she had any; but I was rewarded for my courage by her entranced expression and felt almost grateful to Diane for providing this unique opportunity to get my morale building programme off to a good start. I had to be careful not to lay it on too thick, however, so reverted to her opening remark.

'What, in your view, was so specially fishy about it?'

'Oh, all those daft excuses for not using the telephone. It doesn't cost such a terrible lot to ring London after six o'clock and, anyway, she could have gone to a call box and used her own money; or reversed the charges, if she'd wanted to. Marc would be the last one to complain about that. It just didn't ring true.'

'I agree; and did you notice what a tearing hurry she was in to get away, as soon as you started arguing with her? It seemed to me that she'd been unprepared for that kind of cross-examination. She assumed we'd accept that she was being ultra-thoughtful and leave it at that. There was something else, too.'

'Yes, there was. I bet you all that stuff about having to take her mother to Bexhill is just an excuse for a bit of lead-swinging. She hates having to work in that crummy solicitor's office in Dedley. She's always telling everyone that she feels so stifled and starved of fresh air, but the truth is that she's terrifically lazy.'

'That I wouldn't know, but there's one thing I am able to tell you from first-hand observation. Although she said that her main reason for coming here this morning was to enquire about Geoffrey, it may not have escaped you that, in fact, she never mentioned him again? She scampered away without waiting to find out whether he was alive or dead.'

'Yes, so she did! She's up to something and no mistake. How about steaming that letter open?'

I do not seriously think so ill of myself as to believe that I would have connived in such a disgraceful, undignified trick. I certainly hope not, but I wasn't put to the test because Elsa came in at this point and started to give us the latest news about Geoffrey, which was not particularly encouraging. He was holding his own, according to the hospital report, but still on the danger list and not allowed visitors.

'Did you manage to dig up any relatives?' I asked her.

'Yes, we had a bit of luck there. The poor old boy's methodical ways have finally paid off because there was a stack of letters and packages, all neatly sealed and addressed, but not stamped. Presumably, he collects them up during the week and then takes them in bulk to the post office, as part of the Tuesday morning routine. One of them was addressed to Miss G. Dearing in Somerset who we take to be the sister he visits every spring and autumn.'

'You're right,' Millie said. 'She does live in Somerset. Her name's Gertrude. Don't you remember how Geoffrey took Marc and me to spend a weekend with her when we were quite small? We went by train, so that Geoffrey could point out the special bits of landscape we passed through on the way. It was rather fun and Gertrude was lovely too. She let us pick all the strawberries we could eat and she had a stream running through her garden. But it was only a tiny house, so I stayed with her and Geoffrey and Marc were in a place called the George & Dragon about three miles away. Marc thought that was terrifically grand and grown-up and he boasted about it for ages.'

Elsa looked both saddened and touched by this rare outburst of happy reminiscence and waited a moment or two before saying, 'But I'm sure you don't remember her telephone number, do you? Whereas Geoffrey was obviously far too familiar with it to have bothered to write it in his address book, so now I must try and get hold of her through Directory Enquiries. Failing that, I'll have to send a telegram. We thought of numerous other people who ought to be informed as well, and Louise and I have each made a list of those we'll take on. The Hearnes were on mine, but at least they can be crossed off now.'

'Why?'

'Because I had the luck to meet Diane in the lane just a moment ago. She'd already heard some rumours about Geoffrey and she wanted to know if they were true. She was really worried about him, which rather pleased me. As you know, I have occasionally suspected her of being a tiny bit affected and insincere, but this time there was no mistaking that her concern was genuine.'

Millie was coming on apace. She did not burst a blood vessel or fly into an argument, as I had anticipated. Instead, she merely fanned herself with Diane's letter, giving me an enormous wink over the top of it.

TUESDAY P.M.

The Editor of *The Dedley Mercury* was cautiously co-operative. He was too busy to interview us personally, but offered to send his Features Editor, whose name was Wendy Bright, on Wednesday morning, to gather some information which he might or might not decide to print.

So immediately after lunch, which consisted of embarrassing cutlets for Elsa and me and about four pounds of brown rice for Millie, we set forth to Oak Tree View, which was the rather whimsical and, in the circumstances, sadly ironic name of Geoffrey's cottage.

'I'm afraid he'll have to change that,' I said, as we stood by the sitting room window, looking down at the poor maimed old tree, whose beautiful wide umbrella shape had now been butchered into something more closely resembling a nibbled stick of candy floss. 'No one could possibly take much pleasure from viewing it now, or even recognise it as an oak, come to that.'

Millie had had the brilliant idea of raiding Geoffrey's files for photographs and sketches of the tree in its former glory, of which she knew him to possess dozens, taken from all angles and at all seasons. In this way, she had suggested, we should be able to present a convincing and dramatic set of 'Before' and 'After' pictures, with which to impress Miss Wendy Bright.

The scheme had needed the co-operation of Elsa, whose initial reaction had also been on the cautious side, but, urged on by Millie with exhortations to Think Positive for once, she had eventually given it her blessing and allowed us to borrow the keys.

I could see that in asserting that the tree would grow again I had been foolishly complacent. It might do so one day, but it now seemed inconceivable that this could happen during

Millie's lifetime and, faced with this inescapable truth, the full impact of the wanton destruction hit me with some of the same force which had brought Elsa and the rest of them close to tears. It seemed obvious too that the motive behind it could only have been malice. The hollow was even smaller than I had remembered it and the surrounding land not only was too stony and scrubby to be worth cultivating, but descended so steeply on all sides that its shape was roughly that of a giant teacup, with Oak Tree Cottage making the handle, and surely beyond the power of any tractor or plough to negotiate.

However, I said nothing of this to Millie, who had stood up to her second ordeal with great fortitude and, after staring in silence for something like a minute, had walked over to Geoffrey's filing cabinet, with the set expression of the bereaved leaving the graveside, whose overriding emotion was the dread of having her self-control undermined by expressions of sympathy.

As was to be expected, in view of his neat and methodical habits, all the files were clearly labelled and the contents cross-indexed under subject matter, dates and locations, and it took us less than half an hour to find everything we needed. The next job was to take our own photographs and for this we stationed ourselves at various points in the garden, before moving in towards the fence for some mid-shots.

From there we also had a panoramic view of the surrounding landscape and away over to our right we could make out a solitary female figure slowly picking her way down towards the hollow. We lost sight of her again for a moment or two, as she became obscured from view by the remains of the oak tree, but when she reappeared, on our side of it, we could see that she had blonde hair, was carrying a large carrier bag and wore a brown cardigan over her flowered cotton skirt.

'So she's finished her packing, presumably,' I remarked,

41

'and now she's turned into Cinderella, trudging off to gather up the kindling.'

'Well, she's not likely to find a fairy godmother in the person of Mrs Trelawney.'

'Or her Prince Charming either, I gather. What's he like, by the way?'

'The grandson? Oh, not bad looking and awfully, awfully polite, but I bet he's just as mean and vicious as his rotten old gran underneath all the soapy smarm.'

'And of course he's the one for whose benefit the Hearnes are being turfed out of their house, isn't he? Whereabouts is it?'

'Up there, straight ahead at the top. A little way along from all those ghastly new concrete barns.'

'The white one?'

'No, that's the Macadams'. They've got a freehold, lucky for them. Orchard House is a bit further to the right.'

'Oh yes, I see. It looks quite spacious.'

'Yes, it is; seven or eight bedrooms. I expect they need them with all that brood. Don't you think it's disgusting to clutter up the earth with five children in this day and age?'

'Oh yes, perfectly revolting, but then I suppose you can hardly blame Diane for that. Still, no wonder poor Mrs Hearne gets a bit run down from time to time. What's her husband like?'

'Just as peculiar as she is, in his own way. He's a bit fey, actually. I know that isn't a word you're probably supposed to use about men, but it's the only one I know to describe him. He's always having presentiments and he spends a lot of time communing with the spirits.'

'Doesn't sound as though he'd be much help around the house, though, so perhaps in the end it'll work out for the best. She might be able to cope more efficiently in a smaller place. All the same, it must feel pretty rotten to be kicked out of a house that has been your home for twenty years. And for what? Why should a young man, all on his own, need a house with seven or eight bedrooms?'

'Except that apparently he's planning to get married as soon as he's moved in. To someone terribly posh too, by all accounts, so I suppose he means to turn some of the bedrooms into saunas and stuff like that.'

'Very likely! Who's the intended?'

'No idea. All we know is that he's been boasting about what a terrifically grand family she comes from. So that'll be another feather in the Trelawney cap and she'll probably turn out to be frightfully stuck up and just as horrible as her in-laws.'

'Now, Millie, Think Positive!' I reminded her. 'She may equally well turn out to be perfectly gorgeous and a very mellowing influence.'

'No chance! She'd have to be either horrible or mad to marry into that family.'

There seemed to be no answer to this, so I attempted none and, turning my attention back to the immediate surroundings, saw that Diane had now advanced to the point where she was almost on a level with us and apparently making for the gate in Geoffrey's fence, about a dozen yards from where we were standing. Quiet as we had become by this time, she may have caught the sensation of being observed, for all at once she stopped dead in her tracks, looking down at the ground as intently as though it were transmitting some private message to her, before lifting her head again and meeting our glance. I could not see her face very clearly from that distance, but it struck me that there was something both flustered and annoyed, as well as surprised, in her expression. If so, it was very fleeting and she recovered herself almost immediately, giving a friendly wave of recognition, before clambering on again, up towards the gate.

'This is our very own private short cut,' she explained, rather breathlessly, when she joined us a few seconds later on our side of the fence. 'I've got to pick up some things from the village and Mr Dearing has always been so kind about allowing us to walk through his garden. Goodness, I do hope

43

you won't think it's awful of me to do it when he's not here to give his permission?'

'No, indeed not,' I assured her, packing the camera away in its case, 'I'm perfectly certain he'd want everything to go on exactly the same. And we can give you a lift, if you like? It's practically on our way.'

'Oh, how terribly sweet of you, Tessa! I would be so very grateful,' she exclaimed, sounding quite overwhelmed by this generous offer. 'I suggested to Mummy that it would be such a nice idea to take my aunt some new laid eggs and honey from Mrs Parkinson's shop,' she then explained, having made a great fuss about insisting on taking the back seat, as though this entailed some great sacrifice on her part. 'It will be a little treat for her.'

Ignoring this, Millie said, 'Weren't you afraid of being prosecuted for trespassing, or getting your arms cut off at the elbows?'

'Oh, come on, Millie, it's not as bad as all that, is it?' Diane asked with one of her tinkling laughs.

'Not far off it.'

'Well, you'll say I'm silly, I suppose, but sometimes I wonder if we aren't being a little too hard on them. I mean, I know the old lady can be very difficult and cross, but Daddy told me he'd met Mr Trelawney in the lane this morning and he was really quite upset about the tree; quite shocked, in fact. He assured Daddy that it was done entirely without his knowledge and he's going to try his hardest to make sure nothing worse happens to it.'

'Oh yes? And is turning you out of your house being done entirely without his knowledge, by any chance?'

Diane did not reply to this, but after a moment blew her nose in such a marked manner that even Millie was reduced to silence.

'Do you need a lift home when you've finished your shopping?' I asked.

'Oh, no thank you, Tessa, it's so awfully kind of you, but I couldn't possibly put you to any more trouble,' she replied in a choked voice.

'No trouble at all and if you've got eggs and things to carry....'

'No, no, I'll be quite all right, really I will. The Dedley bus comes through just after four o'clock, so I'll only have a few minutes to wait and it stops at the corner of our lane. It was so good of you to bring me this far and I can't tell you what a help it's been.'

'Deceitful little prig!' Millie muttered, when we had deposited our passenger outside Mrs Parkinson's shop and were turning for home. 'What's she up to now, I wonder?'

'Honestly, Millie, can it be that you're getting an obsession about the wretched girl? Why wouldn't she be taking a present for her aunt? It sounded a perfectly normal thing to me.'

'Well, not to me, it didn't. First of all, she can't afford to make a telephone call to Marcus, who she's supposed to be engaged to, and yet she thinks nothing of loading herself up with Mrs Parkinson's eggs and honey, which is going to set her back quite a packet, I might tell you.'

'Ah, but the difference is, you see, that she's not spending it on herself.'

'Don't tell me you're beginning to be fooled, just like every-one else? I couldn't stand it.'

'No, I agree she's affected and a bit sly as well. I just think you're weakening your case by not allowing her a single redeeming feature.'

'Okay, so what do you say to this? If you hadn't given her a lift, which she certainly can't have been expecting, she couldn't possibly have got to the village a minute before twenty past four, so if she was really intending to go home by bus, how come she didn't leave in time to catch it?'

'You've stumped me there,' I admitted. 'Perhaps I'll come up with the charitable answer when I've given it some thought, but I confess that for the moment it eludes me.'

*

'So how did you two get on?' Elsa asked, filling the kettle from the kitchen tap, and I was reminded both by this and by the reappearance on the table of the banana cake that exactly twenty-four hours had elapsed since my arrival at Pettits Grange. During that short time I had become so embroiled in all the local dramas and personalities that I felt as though I had been there for at least a week.

We gave her a résumé of our afternoon's work, touching on our encounter with Diane and her report of David Trelawney's promise to try and ward off further attacks on the tree, and concluding with the news that some of the photographs had come out rather well.

'Good! Am I not to see them?'

'Oh, blast!' I said. 'I've gone and left them in the car. They're with Geoffrey's, in the pocket of my camera case. I'll fetch it in a minute, but give me a cup of tea first, will you, Elsa, before I collapse?'

'I'll get it,' Millie said, jumping up and running out of the room.

'Honestly, Tessa, I wish you could stay for a month,' Elsa said, looking on in some amazement. 'You seem to have done wonders for Millie already. Imagine dashing off like that, without any nagging at all! And with food on the table, what's more! Considering all this business with Geoffrey and the tree, it's the last sort of mood I'd have expected.'

'What news of Geoffrey, by the way?'

'No news. Condition still unchanged, which is not a good sign, I believe. You notice that Millie didn't even ask? I wish I knew your secret.'

'Nothing very special about it. I find that one infallible way to raise her spirits is to keep remembering to say nasty things about Diane.'

Elsa sighed. 'Yes, I know, and unfortunately that's the one bribe I can't use. The trouble is that I do sympathise, up to a point. She really can be a most irritating girl, but nothing on earth would induce me to admit it to anyone but you. Sooner or later it would get back to her and then it would be all up

46

between Marcus and me. He'd take her side, naturally; one couldn't expect anything else. It makes everything very awkward and I don't know why he had to fall for the one girl his sister can't stand the sight of, but he started looking at Diane when he was about sixteen and he's never really looked away again. As far as I can see, it will be worse than ever when they're married.'

'You think they will be? Millie's hoping he'll come to his senses and tear the wool from his eyes before he becomes irrevocably tangled up in it.'

'That wouldn't solve anything. In fact, I rather pray, for his sake, that it doesn't happen.'

'A bit paradoxical, if I may say so?'

'It's rather hard to explain what I mean, without sounding unbearably snobbish and conceited.'

'That'll be the day!'

'I know our family is no great shakes, but the truth is, Tessa, that Marc would be quite a catch for someone like Diane. He won't be at all badly off, and he's probably clever and presentable enough to do fairly well in his profession. Not bad looking, either, though I do say it! Altogether, it would be quite a step up for little Miss Hearne and, if she's the girl I regret to say I take her to be, she'll cling on, whether he wants her to or not. That being so, I'd like him to have a run for his money, even if only a short one. I'd hate him to become disillusioned even before the wedding and still to be stuck with her for life.'

'Yes, I see what you mean and it's tricky, isn't it? I must ask Toby how he might resolve it in a play. Otherwise, there seems nothing for it but to keep on praying for a miracle.'

Elsa held up her right hand, with two fingers crossed, as Millie re-entered the room, after a somewhat protracted absence. She was empty-handed, but looked strangely triumphant.

'Well?'

'Not there!'

'What do you mean not there? I left it on the back seat.'

'And now it's gone. See for yourself, if you don't believe me.'

'I do believe you, but how can it have gone?'

'Two guesses.'

'You mean. . . ? Oh no, but that's too much! She wouldn't do such a thing, would she?'

'Want to bet?'

'But why, Millie? She's not a kleptomaniac, by any chance?'

'No, not exactly, but she has occasionally been known to borrow things and forget to return them. I expect she wanted to take some pictures of Auntie eating her eggs and honey on the beach at Bexhill. And of course poor, pathetic little Diane couldn't possibly afford to buy a camera of her own, could she now?'

'That's enough, Millie, no need to exaggerate,' Elsa warned her. 'There's probably just been some silly mix-up and we shall find there's a perfectly reasonable explanation.'

'I hope you're right,' I told her, 'and when you find it, do let me be the first to know, will you? We're certainly going to need a good one for Miss Wendy Bright tomorrow morning.'

WEDNESDAY A.M.

The explanation, in my opinion, was neither perfect nor simple, but at least it came promptly. Diane's younger sister, Marigold, telephoned at nine o'clock on Wednesday morning, to pass on a message, of which the gist was as follows:

Diane was most dreadfully sorry but, in all the confusion, she had picked up my camera by mistake. She had not discovered this curious oversight until she was inside the shop and, unfortunately, with all the last minute preparations for an early departure to Bexhill, there had been no time to return it. She had therefore thought it best to leave it in the safe keeping of Mrs Parkinson until it could be collected.

'She sounded relatively sane,' I remarked, having passed on the news to Elsa and Millie. 'A lot less twee and simpering than Diane, at any rate.'

'That's only because she hasn't grown to woman's estate yet. She's not a bad kid, but fairly wonky in her own way. The whole family is.'

'And I must confess that this is just about the wonkiest excuse I ever heard. In all what confusion, I'd like to know? I didn't notice any confusion, did you? And she must have popped it into her shopping bag, otherwise wouldn't we have noticed she was carrying it when she got out of the car?'

'Probably had every intention of pinching it and then lost her nerve,' Millie muttered, with a defiant glance at her mother, who ignored it and said in her peacemaking voice:

'Never mind! The great thing is that we know where it is now, which is all that really matters.'

'Yes, and I'd better get down there right now and retrieve it. If Wendy Bright should be punctual, there isn't a moment to lose.'

'Whatever shall I do, if she turns up before you get back?'

Millie asked in a scared voice.

'Give her some banana cake and ask her a lot of questions about herself and her fascinating career. Interviewers have a secret yearning to become interviewees. Besides, I shan't be long.'

It was a rash promise, though, and it cannot be denied that in my determination not to let her down, I may have driven with something less than my usual staid deliberation. Nevertheless, I apportion the blame for what followed equally between Diane and Mrs Trelawney.

All went swimmingly until I came to the outskirts of the village, where the road straightened out, about a hundred yards short of a fork junction with the Dedley-Storhampton road. Naturally, the traffic on this, and it was normally quite heavy, had right of way and I reduced my fairly considerable speed, in preparation for coming to a complete stop, possibly for half a minute or more, before launching myself into the mainstream. At this point I glanced automatically in the rear mirror and was puzzled and somewhat alarmed to see a powerful white monster of a car, which had been pressed up rather uncomfortably on my back bumper for the past mile or so, now giving signs of intending to overtake me. The headlights were switched on and the right indicator was also flashing its message. There was scarcely enough width at this point to contain two cars and certainly not half the necessary distance ahead for the driver to cut in, in time to stop at the junction. Presuming her, therefore, to be a stranger in these parts, as well as raving mad, I too flashed a warning with my indicator.

This had no effect at all and, with horror and amazement, I saw that the monster had pulled right out and was coming alongside at top speed. I wrenched the steering wheel to the left, towards the sloping grass verge, heard the tearing sound of twigs scratching along the nearside window and got a brief sideways glimpse of a furious female face glaring into mine, just a second before I felt the car tilting over and was obliged to give my whole attention to bracing myself for it to topple sideways into the road. It righted itself in the nick of time and I came to a dead stop at last, although still at a somewhat precarious angle, half on and half off the bank.

I was so shocked and frightened that I knew that if I attempted to climb out it would be I who toppled over and, furthermore, that by opening my door, or even clambering across to the nearside one, I could well upset the delicate balance and precipitate the very disaster I had so far managed to avert. So I stayed where I was and waited for the Samaritan to arrive.

He did so surprisingly quickly, for in a matter of seconds a station wagon drew up behind me and a man got out and walked up to my window. It was our second meeting in somewhat fraught circumstances and the twitch and the palm rubbing were both in action.

'Oh, hallo!' I said feebly. 'How's your dog?'

'Not too good, I'm afraid. We'll probably have to . . . but listen, what about you? Are you all right?'

'Never less so. Would you mind propping up the car while I climb out?'

'Yes, of course. You shouldn't have any trouble, if you take it slowly. It's probably not as bad as it feels.'

'It could hardly be worse than it feels.'

'That's partly shock, you know, and I sympathise. I saw what happened.'

'Oh, good! I may call on you to explain to Robin that those scratches weren't my fault. You didn't get that fiend's number, by any chance?'

'No need to. I can so easily find it out.'

'I may have concussion,' I told him, 'because I don't quite follow you.'

'Quite simple; all too simple and familiar, in fact. I recognised the car, not to mention the driver. She had overtaken me a minute or two before.'

'And you recognised her? Are you sure?'

'Oh dear me, yes, no question about that!' he said in his

sour way, followed by a particularly violent spasm of the facial muscles.

'How extraordinary!'

'You wouldn't say so, if you lived here. It's the kind of behaviour we've come to expect. How are you feeling, by the way?'

'Recovered, thanks. In a fighting mood, in fact. Do you think I should report her to the police?'

'You could try, I suppose, but I wouldn't reccommend it personally.'

'Why not? You saw what she did? If that doesn't add up to driving without due care and attention, I'd like to know what does.'

'Oh, admittedly, but I have to point out that apart from a few scratches, which could have been made anywhere and at any time, there's no damage to show for it, so it would just be our word against hers and, unfortunately, I'm not what you'd call an impartial witness. The police might believe us, but I doubt if there's much they could do about it.'

'I expect you're right,' I agreed, 'and, anyway, I haven't time for vengeance now. There is much to be done and done fast, if I am not to let the side down. Could you be very kind and help me push the car on to the road, before I risk getting in again?'

'Very well, I'll push and you steer.'

'Incidentally,' I added, after thanking him, 'you didn't finish telling me about Daisy. How is she?'

'In pretty bad shape. One leg's completely paralysed and the vet doesn't hold out much hope of her getting the use of it back.'

'Oh, how rotten for you!'

'Yes, it's a bad blow. It wouldn't matter so much if she wasn't a sporting dog, but it wouldn't be fair to let a game old creature like her drag out the rest of her life on three legs. It looks as though there's nothing for it but to have her put down.'

'I am sorry. And of course that's something else to be laid

52

at the door of the demon driver, isn't it?'

He looked puzzled, perhaps even faintly alarmed for a moment, then his expression cleared and he said, 'Oh, I see what you mean. Yes, indeed; and another instance where the police appear to be powerless, moreover. No use relying on them, I fear, to rid us of this hellish persecution.'

Having said this, Tim put his handkerchief over his mouth, as though he had received warning of a particularly violent muscular twitch, then turned away and walked back to his car, evidently too distressed even to wish me goodbye.

It was past ten o'clock by the time I reached Mrs Parkinson's combined shop and tea room, now open for morning coffee and homemade cakes, which meant more delay ahead.

There were three customers squashed up round one of the little gate-legged oak tables and the proprietress, an imposing female, wearing a flowered overall and looking as though she had rather let herself go on her own pastries, was taking their order. So I had to wait until that was over and then go through all the business of explaining that I had not come to eat or drink, but simply to collect a camera.

'Oh yes, of course, it's safe and sound in my office. It's Miss Crichton, isn't it? Diane said you'd be calling for it. To tell you the truth, we weren't sure whether she was having us on, but, naturally, I recognise you now. What an honour, though! I wonder if you'd mind sitting down for just a tick while I cope with this order and then I'll fetch it for you? Shan't be a mo, but I'm short-handed this morning.'

So I sat at one of the tables, seething with impatience, for another ten minutes, until at last she was able to give me her attention again.

'Oh, thank you so much,' I said, leaping up and practically seizing the camera out of her hand. 'And now could you possibly direct me to the nearest call box?'

'Well, let's think now. Quite a long way, I'm afraid. I really believe the post office would be about your nearest. You know where the post office is?'

'No, but I hope it's not far? I've got rather an urgent call to make.'

'In that case, Miss Crichton, why ever not use this one?' she asked, pointing to the glass show case and counter. 'I take it you're not going to have a long chat with someone in Hollywood?' she added archly.

'No, no, just a local number.'

'Then be my guest! I think that's the expression, isn't it?'

'Absolutely! And thanks a million!'

'This is me,' I announced when Millie answered. 'Has your friend arrived yet?'

There was no way of telling whether the three customers were tourists or local people, and Mrs Parkinson was staring out of the window with that expression on her face which told the world that nothing was further from her mind than the desire to eavesdrop on other people's telephone conver-sations, so I thought it prudent to keep it cryptic. Unfortun-ately, I was unable to explain this to Millie, who said dazedly, 'What friend?'

'Oh, you know, the one you were expecting at ten o'clock. Has she come yet?'

'No, she hasn't.'

'Really? She's late then. Still, that's a bit of luck. This is just to let you know that I'll be back in ten minutes.'

'Don't burst yourself. She's not coming.'

'What do you mean not coming?'

'They rang up about five minutes after you left. It was the Editor's secretary. She said I was to tell you that the appointment had to be cancelled. The reporter who was coming to see us has been called away on another job and they can't spare anyone else.'

'Didn't she suggest another appointment?'

'No, she said that was all she knew about it. Where are you, anyway?'

'In a trance, actually. There's been some dirty work here, you know, and we must find out what's behind it. And since, after all, there's no hurry, I'll get started on it here and now. Expect me in half an hour.'

The reason for this change of strategy was that, while talking, I had seen the morning coffee party signalling to Mrs Parkinson for their bill, which was not readily forthcoming, so absorbed was she in her own thoughts and the view down the High Street. However, as I had forseen, she promptly returned to the everyday world as soon as I put the receiver back and, by making a drawn out business of searching for some imaginery object in my bag, I contrived matters so that she and I had the place to ourselves.

'Thank you so much, Mrs Parkinson. My mind is now at rest and it turned out not to be so urgent, after all. In fact, I really believe I've time for a cup of coffee. Would that be possible?'

'It certainly would. How about some scones and jam to help it go down?'

'No thanks, just coffee would be lovely.'

'Of course, you might know there wouldn't be a cat in the place the one time we have a celebrity on view,' she remarked, setting the tray down a few minutes later.

Fervently hoping that all the cats would stay away for just a little longer, I said, 'How very kind of you, but in fact I feel rather silly sitting here all alone. Won't you join me?'

'I'm tempted, sorely tempted, but better not, thanks ever so much. It wouldn't look too good if anyone should come in. Not that we ever get more than a handful, as a rule, on Wednesdays. For one thing, it's early closing, you see. That's why Shirley, my assistant, has that as her day off. Not really enough for two of us to do.'

'But she was here yesterday, when Diane brought my camera in?'

'Oh, she was and she was thrilled to bits. I can't think what she's going to say when I tell her you were in this morning. Go through the roof, I shouldn't wonder. She'd seen you on the box only the other week, you see. But perhaps you'll be back? How long are you stopping in these parts, if it's not a rude question?'

'About a week, probably. I'm staying with Mrs Carrington at Pettits Grange.'

'Yes, I know. Diane told us that too.'

'Did she?' I asked idly. 'What else did she tell you?'

'Oh, all sorts of things and, of course, Shirl was egging her on. About how she'd met you, quite by chance, when you were taking photographs of the local beauty spots, and then you'd given her a lift into the village and there'd been this muddle about the camera and I don't know what all. She goes on a bit, but she is a nice girl, that Diane, isn't she? No side at all and always so considerate and polite. A bit scatty, of course, but then they all are, that family. I mean, who in the world except one of the Hearnes would walk off with someone else's camera, without realising what they'd done? We all had a good laugh about that, after she'd gone.'

'So no customers queueing up yesterday either? Well, I suppose it must have been getting towards closing time, by then?'

'No, not quite, but yesterday was rather slack, as it happens, specially considering it's August. We normally get quite a few hikers and such, this time of year, but there were only two customers here when Diane came in.'

'Hikers?'

'Oh no, local people they were, waiting for the Dedley bus. Going to the cinema, they said. Movies, as they call them now. Nice young couple and great fans of yours too, you'll be glad to hear.'

'Yes, I'm delighted. In fact, I'm doing one of those television panel games next month, and if you'll give me their names I'll send them some tickets for the recording, to show my appreciation.'

'Would you really? Jim and Sue Baldwin, they're called. He's from the Midlands somewhere, but she's been here all her life. Her mother works up at Mrs Trelawney's, who bought Pettits Farm not so long ago. That's the big house in these parts, as you probably know. Jim and Sue have got a bungalow on the new Carfax estate. Can't remember the number offhand, but if you send the letter here I'll make sure they get it. And coffee's on the house, by the way. No, truly, I wouldn't dream of charging you. I've enjoyed our little chat.'

'So have I,' I assured her, 'very much indeed.'

'Honestly, Tessa, you do have the most staggering luck! Imagine finding all that out in about a quarter of an hour; with a free cup of coffee thrown in.'

'It wasn't purely luck, as it happens, Millie,' I replied, rather stung.

'Well, I bet nothing like it would have come my way, if I'd sat there gorging scones and cakes the whole morning.'

'That's partly because you're not nosey and partly because neither are you an actress.'

'You mean that people let their hair down with you because they know you are one?'

'Yes, sometimes they do, I believe, but it isn't only that. I'm sure nearly all actors acquire the habit of watching the way people walk and of listening to how they talk and so on. It becomes like second nature and you find yourself switching on almost as a matter of course. Mrs Parkinson is quite a character, in her way, and at the same time she belongs to a type which most people would recognise and place right away. In other words, first class material. So I was paying careful attention to everything she said.'

'And what did she say?'

'I can't remember the exact words, but the implication was quite clearly that she had not been alone in the shop when Diane brought the camera in. I remembered that as soon as you told me on the telephone that Wendy Bright hadn't come, wouldn't be coming and that the enterprise had been shelved, if not abandoned completely.'

'Why? What's that got to do with Mrs Parkinson not being alone in the shop?'

'Well, don't you see, Millie, we have to face the fact that

our Editor has been nobbled. Word must have reached the enemy that we were planning this coup and immediate counter action has been taken. She probably threatened the poor man with some gigantic libel suit, if he dared to print a word of it. So the question was: whence came the leak? Naturally, when Mrs Parkinson was referring to "we" and "us", I concluded she meant simply that Shirley, her assistant, had been there and I intended to concentrate on her and find out whether there was any link there with Mrs Trelawney, but before I even got started on that Mrs Parkinson gave me another clue and this time I do remember her exact words. She said: "We all had a good laugh about that after she", meaning Diane, "had gone". That was really much more promising because it opened up the field a lot and gave me something to work on. It wasn't all that difficult either because, today being Wednesday, business was slack and she was quite keen to detain me for as long as possible. Anyway, it's obvious that Jim or Sue must be the missing link. No doubt, one of them described the episode to Sue's mother, who promptly passed it on to her employer.'

'Yes, but, Tessa, how could the old cow have guessed what we were going to use the photographs for? Even blabby old Diane didn't know that. At least . . . you didn't tell her, did you?'

'No, certainly not, and it's a safe bet that it would never have occurred to her what their real purpose was, but I'm also willing to bet that at some point, while they were all giggling and gossiping in the tea shop, one of them took the photographs out and they all had a look. Now, if you remember, we'd put each set into a separate envelope? Yours, which you took from Geoffrey's files, were labelled Before and my new ones went into the After envelope. That might not have suggested anything in particular to the Parkinson gang, but don't you agree that when Mrs Trelawney heard about it she'd have caught on in a flash? From there, but a step, as they say, to figuring out how we intended to use them.'

'Yes, I suppose so,' Millie said gloomily. 'She's no fool, I do realise. Not clever in any sort of way that matters, but definitely cunning. So what do we do now?'

'We could try some of the other local papers, I daresay, but I doubt if there'd be much point. *The Mercury* is the quality one in these parts and probably has the biggest circulation, but I don't suppose Mrs Trelawney was taking any chances. She's probably delivered her ultimatum to every editor for miles around. Still, we won't accept defeat yet, will we? There must be some other way to get our message across. I might consult Toby on that. He can be very cunning too, in his way. In the meantime, Millie, let's take a proper look at the photographs and decide which arrangement makes the most telling effect.'

Elsa joined us while we were laying them out on the table like patience cards, except that it turned out to bear more resemblance to a hand of piquet, because Millie had ten cards in her envelope, whereas mine contained only seven.

I stared at them for a moment, then counted again to make absolutely sure.

'Now what's the matter?' Elsa asked.

'One missing. There were eight left on the roll and I used it all up.'

'How mysterious!'

'Baffling, I'd call it.'

'Which one is it?' Millie asked.

'How would I know, when it's not there to tell me?'

'Do you suppose one of them pinched it?'

'Presumably; but why, for God's sake? They were all photo-graphs of the tree and the only variations were in distances and angles. So what would be the point of taking just one? Why not the lot?'

'Because then you'd have just gone out and taken eight more.'

'Yes, that's true; whereas they thought I might not notice if only one were missing. Clever Millie! Only it still doesn't explain anything really. What earthly use would one photograph be to anyone?'

'Some form of counter-attack, maybe? To prove that you were trespassing?'

'Only we weren't, were we? We never set foot outside Geoffrey's garden.'

'One way and another,' Elsa remarked, 'you don't seem to be making much headway with this enterprise. Perhaps you had better call it off and try something else?'

Millie sighed. 'Isn't that just typical? One set-back and you're ready to drop everything!'

'Besides,' I added, 'we have at least succeeded in drawing the enemy's fire and that can't be nothing. It probably indicates that we're moving in the right direction.'

'And where does the right direction lead you next?' Elsa asked, a trifle smugly.

Which, I was bound to admit, was the big question.

WEDNESDAY P.M.

In the hope of gathering some information which might provide at least part of the answer, I set forth at about three o'clock that afternoon for a personal inspection of the Trelawney headquarters, which, despite the fact that the name had now been officially changed to Sowerley Manor, was still known throughout the neighbourhood as Pettits Farm.

Millie was engaged to take part in an anti-nuclear protest rally on the steps of Dedley Town Hall the following morning and was required to spend the whole of Wednesday afternoon helping her group to assemble the banners and run through their chants, and Elsa, for whom the dictates of conscience were wrapped in a different sort of package, had left soon after lunch to dole out jelly and buns at the monthly gathering of the Darby and Joan club. Since I had a particular and personal curiosity concerning Mrs Trelawney, in addition to the general one, this seemed to be the ideal opportunity to indulge it.

Unwilling to risk my car in the danger zone, after its recent narrow squeak, I walked along the lane in the opposite direction from the village until I came to the mud and grass track known as Pettits Row. This in fact provided access only to the Big House, some fifty yards ahead, after which it narrowed into a footpath and short cut to a nearby village, and I saw that there was now a brand new notice board standing squarely on each side of the entrance. One stated that there was No Through Road, the other that Trespassers Would Be Prosecuted.

Presumably, Mrs Trelawney had been restrained from actually declaring it to be private property, but no stranger to the neighbourhood could have guessed that it had been a

61

public right-of-way for about a thousand years and remained so to this day.

Not being one myself, I proceeded on to the house and, once the shock of confronting the new wall had subsided a little, my first thought was that Elsa had understated the case. It was even higher then I had visualised it and the bricks were not so much bright red as purplish liver coloured. It was hard to believe that any sane person could have erected such a barrier between herself and the world, or could have remained so after living behind it for more than a few days.

About half way along this wall there was a high, wide, but far from handsome wrought iron gate, arch shaped and fringed at the top with long spikes. There was a padlock attached to it by a heavy iron chain, although this, surprisingly, was unfastened, and I stood for a few minutes, peering through the tiny gaps in the bars and curlicues at the scene beyond.

It was not an edifying one. The house, which lay straight ahead, at the end of a short tarmac drive, had been painted white and the ancient supporting beams, formerly a warm light brown in colour, had been picked out in black varnish. The roof had also been brought up to date and the old, mellow looking tiles replaced by grey slate.

Nailed to the gate was yet another notice board, this one warning me to Beware of the Dog, and the big white car stood facing me at the side of the house. I could almost believe that it was sneering and snorting at me with personal malevolence, but on the other hand I could not hear or see any dog and, managing to convince myself that not even this car was capable of roaring down the drive and running me over, without human guidance, I turned the heavy iron ring and walked slowly up towards this vulgar and pretentious fortress.

The reason for the slow pace was partly to give myself time to work out the next move, partly in the confident hope of attracting the attention of someone inside, so that the initiative would be taken out of my hands. This gambit did not come off, however, and, contrary to expectations, nothing and no one interfered with my progress to the front door.

It was a particularly hideous and inappropriate one, being made of thick, opaque, ribbed glass, set into a modern wood frame. I pushed the bell button and heard the chimes jingling through the house and, in a matter of seconds, the door was opened, though only by a foot or so, by a faded little middle-aged woman, who, being so patently not Mrs Trelawney, was presumably Sue Baldwin's mother. She had evidently been on the point of going out, because she wore a scarf round her head and was holding a large brown bag.

'Is Mrs Trelawney in?'

'Yes . . . I believe so, but I'm sorry. . . . You're not from the Council, are you?'

It was tempting to claim that I was, but I could see that ultimately this would only add another hurdle to those which lay ahead, so I said, 'No, this is just a social call.'

'Then I'm sorry, Miss, but she won't see you. Mrs Trelawney never sees anyone without they have an appointment.'

I was debating whether to tell her I had one, when my quarry appeared in person, a tall, gaunt looking woman, who loomed up in the background and then, roughly pushing her minion aside, flung the door wide open and said in a loud voice, which still retained traces of an Australian accent, 'Who's there, Alice, and what do they want?'

'Beg pardon, Ma'am, but I don't know who it is. Some young lady, as you see. I opened the door, seeing as you were expecting someone from the Council. . . .'

'Yes, all right, I'll deal with it. You can get off home now. And don't forget to leave the gate unlocked. Mr David will see to it later.'

Then, turning to me, she barked, 'If you're not from the Council, who are you and what do you want?'

'To see you, if you can spare me a few minutes?'

'Nothing doing. I don't see anyone unless they've been invited. Didn't Alice tell you that?'

63

'Yes, she did, but the fact is that you have seen me now, so I don't see what difference another two minutes could make.'

'You can let me be the judge of that, if you don't mind. I don't have any truck with strangers and if you're selling something the answer is no, I don't want it.'

'I'm not selling anything and I'm not quite a stranger. We have met before, as it happens.'

'That so?' she asked, peering at me more closely. 'Not as I recall, young lady.'

'Well, it was some time ago. In Stratford, Ontario.'

'Oh yes?'

'I had a walk-on and understudy in *School for Scandal.* You were called Mrs Carew in those days and you were a lot more hospitable too. You gave a party for the whole cast, on the evening before we left. It was a very good party, as a matter of fact, very lavish.'

'Thanks. What's your name?'

'Theresa Crichton.'

'Yes, got it now. Reason being you wrote me a letter. Straight out of the book of etiquette, I remember. Oh well, come in, if you must, but only for a minute or two, mind! I'm a very busy woman.'

'So I hear,' I told her, getting a sharp look in return. She did not comment, however, but marched ahead of me into a room leading off the hall, which managed to look both ostentatious and austere in the same breath. The old sash windows had been replaced by the modern, single pane variety, there was an electric fire, with plastic logs in the inglenook fireplace, a sunburst clock over the brick chimney piece and the upholstery and curtains were putty coloured throughout, with carpet and cushions to tone. The single bright spot was an enlarged colour photograph, which had a place to itself on a table between two of the windows. It showed my hostess standing with arms linked between a fair-haired young man and a dark, good-looking girl, wearing jodphurs and a crimson jersey. All three were beaming at the camera and even Mrs Trelawney looked amiable. It

64

provided a much needed human touch.

'What are you up to now?' she enquired, busying herself with a glass cigarette box and a Wedgwood table lighter the size of a football, 'Still acting?'

'Yes,' I replied in a pained voice.

The unspoken reproach was not lost on her and she said, 'Oh, don't mind me, I wouldn't know about such things. Never go inside a theatre nowadays, if I can avoid it. It was Mr Carew, my late husband, who was stage struck. He'd have dragged me there every night during the season, if he'd had his way. Shaw, Shakespeare, you name it! I used to be nearly crying with boredom half the time. Still, your little effort wasn't as bad as some of them, I seem to remember. And I expect you get a big kick out of showing off like that, night after night, don't you?'

'Yes, if you put it like that, I suppose I do.'

'Don't know what other way you could put it. Still, that's neither here nor there. What I want to know is what you think you're doing here now? You haven't come to thank me all over again for a party I gave four years ago, that's for sure!'

'No.'

'Why, then?'

'Mainly curiosity, I'm afraid.'

'Well, I'll be . . . Still, at least that's honest, I suppose. What, may I ask, did you want to know?'

'When you nearly knocked me and my car off the road this morning I recognised you as someone I'd met, although at the time I couldn't place it. In fact, I didn't try very hard, I had other things on my mind. Then soon afterwards I learnt that you were the famous, or infamous, Mrs Trelawney, which didn't seem to connect, so I thought perhaps I'd been mistaken.'

'I remarried soon after Mr Carew died. Must have been not long after you were over there that time.'

'And Mr Trelawney is also now dead, I understand?'

'Divorced, as it happens, although I don't know what business it is of yours?'

'None whatever, but from the moment I arrived here I've been hearing these tales about the eccentric and mischievous behaviour of Mrs Trelawney and, when I found out that she was you, I was puzzled. Somehow I couldn't easily reconcile all that senseless destruction with the woman I thought I'd recognised in the car. Of course, I'd only met you on that one occasion in Ontario, but I still found it hard to accept the idea that I'd been mistaken, because one clear memory I had about the one in Canada was her Australian accent. It was probably much more noticeable there than in this country, where we've all grown accustomed to it. Anyway, the plain truth is that I couldn't wait to find out whether you were the same person or not.'

'Is that so? Well, at least you've been frank about it, which is more than you can say for most of the crowd round here. Satisfied now?'

'Not absolutely. I'd still be interested to know why you picked an out of the way place like this to come and live in, where you had no roots and no friends.'

'Oh, you would, would you? And I'd be interested to know how long it'll be before I tell you to mind your own business. Still, if you must know, I didn't exactly pick it, it kind of picked me.'

'Did it really?'

'Yes, really. Five or six years ago it would be. My late husband had an honorary degree conferred on him by one of those Oxford colleges. He was dead chuffed about it and we decided to stay over for an extra few days and explore the countryside. This part of the world was on our route and it sort of grabbed me. Love at first sight, you might say. I've had cause to regret it once or twice since.'

I could believe this, and also that either the late husband had been at the wheel during most of this excursion, or that her style of driving had deteriorated considerably since those days, if she had really been able to focus attention on her

66

surroundings sufficiently to have retained these affectionate memories.

Aloud I said, 'Well, one final question, if you'll bear with me? Why then, having returned here and turned the dream into reality, did you promptly set about doing everything in your power to ruin it, thereby causing havoc and misery to a number of people who've lived in these parts for donkey's years and have never done you the slightest harm?'

'So that's the story, is it? Well, you may as well know, girl, that you've been led up the garden. The truth is that I tried like fury to be friendly when I first came here. It had stuck in my mind as the kind of nice, peaceful place where I'd be happy to end my days, and maybe do a bit of good into the bargain. I knew I had to tread carefully though. Just throwing money around wouldn't get me anywhere. But there was a lot needed doing, I could see that, and a lot of the power had got into the wrong hands. All those rural preservation societies and what-have-you, for a start. Lot of old fuddy-duddies, with not a new idea between them. I did my best to shake them up a bit, inject some new life, I really flogged myself to death over it, and what happened? Turned up their noses and made it clear they didn't want to know, that's what! They'd been pottering along like this for a couple of centuries and that was good enough for them. No winds of change to blow round here, if you don't mind! There now, I don't suppose you've been allowed to see it from the other side, have you? Well, no skin off my nose and I can't imagine what right you think you have to come barging into a person's private property and asking them to account for themselves. This place belongs to me now and I can do as I choose with it. The sooner that's understood the better.'

'I am sure it is understood, but I still think it could land you in trouble. You know what they say about no man being an island?'

'No, I don't know what they say, Miss Clever, and I don't care. Now, are you going to pick yourself up off that chair and get out of here, or aren't you?'

'Right away,' I told her, getting up, 'and I'm sorry to have annoyed you. That really wasn't my intention.'

'Don't you worry! Pinpricks like this don't annoy me. And you can go back and tell all those snooty friends of yours, who I take it sent you up here to threaten or plead, which-ever it was, that they'll have to get up a bit earlier in the morning to catch me napping.'

'You're mistaken. No one sent me. It was entirely my own idea.'

'And not a very bright one, in my opinion. And now, if you'll excuse me, I've got someone coming to see me.'

'Yes, I know,' I said, moving towards the door. 'Someone from the Council, I believe? I hope he gets a warmer reception than I did.'

'Oh, I shan't stand any nonsense from him, don't fret!'

'No, I won't. In fact, if anyone needs to be fretted about, I'd say it was you. You're the one I feel sorry for,' I told her grandly, taking care to shoot out of the room before she could cap it.

Later that afternoon I telephoned Toby to enquire how the play was coming along.

'I haven't started to write it yet. This is simmering and meditation time. It can go on for months.'

'So I've noticed. And, talking of simmering, is Mrs Parkes back yet?'

'Not until the weekend.'

'Oh, what a nuisance for you!'

'And for her too, I sincerely trust. Just imagine her in Weston-super-Mare, with nothing to eat but frozen cod sub-stitute and soggy chips! The thought of it is practically the only thing that keeps me going.'

'Although I daresay your own diet is no great improve-ment. How about coming over to lunch tomorrow? Millie will be out all day with the marchers, so we shan't be made to feel like ravening carnivores if we toy with a lamb chop.'

'Yes, all right, I might do that. Any new developments to

go into my simmering pot?'

'A little headway here and there. I feel I'm getting close to finding out which snub caused the chip on the Trelawney shoulder, although it's not particularly original. You may need to invent something more startling. However, events move so fast around here that I may well have more to tell you by tomorrow. Such as the solution to the missing photograph, for instance.'

'That doesn't sound very promising either. At this rate, I may be forced to give up the whole idea.'

'Oh, come now! You only feel like that because you're a little undernourished at present and, God knows, I'm doing my best for you, so let's not despair! See you tomorrow about one.'

Elsa arrived home soon after this and I told her what I had done.

'Oh yes?' she replied in an abstracted tone.

'You don't sound very enthusiastic.'

'Oh, it's not that. I'm always delighted to see Toby, as you know. It's just that I'm feeling a little sad and upset at the moment.'

'Oh dear! Why's that?'

'Geoffrey died early this morning.'

'Oh, my dearest Elsa, I am sorry! Did he . . . was he. . . ?'

'Yes, quite peaceful. His sister was with him. She arrived yesterday and Tim and Louise are putting her up. She's going home this evening and the funeral will be in Somerset. So it wouldn't really have made any difference if she'd stayed there all the time because he never regained conciousness, poor old boy.'

'I am so sorry,' I said again.

'Perhaps it's all for the best, really. He couldn't have gone on living in the cottage on his own and he'd have hated being dependent. Solitude and self-sufficiency meant so much to him. It's sad, nonetheless, and if there's any justice in this world, God forgive me, but I can't help hoping that Mrs Trelawney will pay for this some day. He was always so gentle and kind and we shall miss him dreadfully.'

We were both silent for a while and then Elsa said, 'You'll probably accuse me of being fussy and over-protective, but I'd be grateful if you didn't say anything of this to Millie just yet. I do realise that she'll have to be told very soon, but she's so looking forward to this march, or whatever it is they're going on tomorrow and I'd hate anything to spoil it for her.'

'Okay, I won't say a word. How does she get to Dedley, by the way? Has she got her driving licence?'

'No, not yet. She can't take the test until she's seventeen.'

'So you have to drive her there?'

'Oh, good heavens, no, that wouldn't do at all. She would never live down the shame of it. No, there are about twenty of them going from around here and they've hired a coach. It's to pick them up in the village at ten o'clock and she can get as far as there on her bike.'

However, before Millie arrived in Dedley the next morning, perhaps even before she had boarded the coach, some news had broken which would have gone a very long way towards consoling her, even for the loss of her beloved Geoffrey.

THURSDAY A.M.

The messenger was Louise Macadam, who burst into the kitchen while we were finishing breakfast and, if she had been Joris making a brief stop-over between Ghent and Aix, she could not have been in a wilder state of excitement.

She was a short, unattractively squat sort of woman, with cropped grey hair, a little too elderly looking to match her face, and was shabbily dressed in clothes which had been expensive when they were bought, far too many moons ago. From the absence of lines and wrinkles, I assumed that she normally wore a calm and impassive expression, which was certainly not the case when she breezed in on Thursday morning. Elsa, undoubtedly, was startled by something out of the way in her appearance, for she said with some alarm, 'Louise! My dear, whatever's the matter? Are you all right?'

'Perfectly, thanks. Just a little out of breath and dying for some coffee, if you can spare a cup? I couldn't bear to waste a single minute before telling you the news, and I couldn't ring up because the police are still there and they asked me to leave the line free and to tell any callers to ring back later.'

'The police? In your house? What for? Have you had a burglary or something?'

'No, nothing like that, they wanted to see Alice. You know, Alice Hawkins, who comes to me two mornings a week. It used to be four until the old witch enticed her away with offers of fairy gold,' she added in parenthesis.

'What did they want to see Alice about?' Elsa asked, getting up to fetch a cup and saucer, her first blaze of curiosity now somewhat dimmed. 'What's she been up to? Not shoplifting, I hope?'

'No, no, they just wanted to ask her a few questions.'

'What about?'

'My dear, if you'll only allow me to get a word in edgeways, I'll tell you. It's precisely why I've come,' Louise said, and the hint of impatience in her words and tone struck an unexpected note, because Elsa had given an enthusiastic build-up for her only the day before, impressing upon me what a brave and saintly woman she was, forever doing good by stealth and hiding her light under a bushel. The feeling was now growing that she hid it a sight too cunningly, for I had noticed that she had a brusque, decidedly ungracious manner and, particularly when it fell on me, a cold and fishy eye behind the strong lensed spectacles.

'And I must explain that I only happen to be in the know because poor Alice was so terrified that she went completely to pieces and could hardly utter a word. They tried their best to explain that they weren't about to drag her off to prison, only wanted some information, but it didn't make a hoot of difference. In the end they called me in to try and calm her down a bit, which I was able to do and after that they allowed me to stay for the whole interview.'

'But you said they were still there?'

'Yes, yes, and so they were when I left, but only while one of them typed out a statement for Alice to sign. They'd promised that once this was done they'd leave her in peace and I told her to go straight home. There wouldn't be the slightest hope of getting any work out of her, after a drama like this. And, anyway, the silver can go for once, now that it looks as though I may be having her back for four mornings a week once again,' Louise added with a certain relish.

'Why? You don't mean to tell me that Mrs Trelawney is leaving us, by any chance? No, what am I talking about? That wouldn't be a police matter. Exactly what do you mean, Louise? Has something happened to her?'

'Oh, indeed it has! The ultimate and most incredible thing in the world has happened to her. Mrs Trelawney has been murdered!'

Elsa's cup clattered on to the saucer and she gripped the edge of the table, sitting stiff and rigid with shock for almost a minute.

'Who ... by?' she asked at last, in something near to a whisper.

'Burglars, caught in the act, or so it appears. She'd been stabbed to death in her own drawing room.'

'I see! Had they taken much?'

'Well, as far as I remember, there was a transistor radio missing, also a table lighter and a couple of other trifles, I really forget now; but the hi-fi equipment and a clock, among other things, were stacked up by the front door, so it looked as though they must have been interrupted when they were half way through the job, lost their heads and killed her and then made a bolt for it, leaving most of the stuff behind. Isn't it just the weirdest and most fantastic thing you ever heard of?'

'Yes. Yes, it is.'

'Although, as the Inspector rather gloomily pointed out, it is something that happens all too frequently nowadays to elderly women alone in their houses.'

'Somehow, I would never have expected it to happen to this one.'

'Nor would I,' I admitted.

Louise glanced at me with the air of one noticing the presence of a third party for the first time, which was partially excusable because in the heat of the moment Elsa had evidently forgotten that we had never met.

'Oh, forgive me, both of you!' she now said and proceeded to wade through the introductions.

'How do you do, Tessa? What was it you said?'

'Nothing of importance. What I'd really be interested to know is what time this happened?'

'Between four o'clock, when Alice left, and about seven-thirty, as far as I could make out.'

'Who found her?'

'David, the grandson; when he came in from the farm.'

'Not until seven-thirty? He was rather late home, wasn't he?'

'Not particularly. They're very busy with the harvest at this time of year, you know.'

I had been on the point of saying that I had nevertheless gained the impression that Mrs Trelawney had been expecting him back earlier than that, but recollected myself in time and asked instead, 'How long had she been dead when he found her.'

'I'm afraid I have no idea.'

Louise was beginning to look rather put out by all these questions and Elsa said soothingly, 'You mustn't mind Tessa. She's one of our geminis.'

'Really? And what does that mean?'

'It means she leads a double life. As well as being a successful actress, she's been mixed up in a lot of detective work in her time. Also her husband is a member of Scotland Yard, so she has a more professional approach than the rest of us.'

Whether it was the acting or the detecting which displeased her I could not tell, but obviously Louise found the information somewhat distasteful. Perhaps Elsa noticed this too, for she went on quickly, 'The question I'd like to ask is this: how in the world did this gang, or whoever they were, manage to break in? I'd always understood that the place was bolted and barred against all intruders, even those with no evil intent?'

'So it is, as a rule, but yesterday was the big exception. That was where Alice was such a help and it just shows how right they were to persevere until they got her to talk. You see, normally when she leaves at four she's supposed to lock the main gate after her. It's on a padlock and she and Mrs Trelawney and David each had a key, but yesterday Mrs Trelawney reminded her to leave it open because she was expecting someone from the Council. There now, isn't that something? You can imagine the gleam in the Inspector's eye when she came up with that bit of news.'

'Yes, indeed! Was she able to add anything to it? Any details about this visitor?'

'No, none at all, and not surprisingly.'

'Oh?'

'Because, my dear, and this is the really fascinating part, it was obviously a hoax. The minute the Inspector heard about it he was on the telephone to his office, instructing under-lings to ring up the Council immediately and get every scrap of information they could about this appointment, including the name and business of the officer in question. About twenty minutes later they rang back to say that there'd been no appointment and no such officer existed. Naturally, he didn't repeat this to Alice and me, but you could tell from his end of the conversation that that was what it amounted to, and you can see what it must mean?'

'No, not exactly.'

'That this was definitely not the work of a bunch of thugs or hooligans who just happened to be lurking about and just happened to find the gate unlocked. It must have been very carefully planned by someone who knew all the ins and outs of the household. In other words, one assumes, a local person, with the knowledge and intelligence to invent such a pretext for getting in. Presumably, the intention was to tie her up and gag her while they were on the job, but things must have got out of hand for some reason. Well, of course, that was the attitude the Inspector took when he was talking to Alice, but it didn't fool me for one minute. I'm pretty sure he believes, as I do, that she was killed deliberately and that the so-called burglary was just a blind.'

Elsa did not appear particularly elated to hear this. 'But they have no idea at all who it could have been?' she asked doubtfully.

'I imagine not. As I say, he wasn't giving any more away than he could help, naturally; but what I say is, do we honestly want him to find out? That may be an awful thing to say, but personally I feel nothing but gratitude and, provided it doesn't become a habit, I shan't waste any sleep if they get away with it.'

'I understand perfectly how you feel, Louise, and it would be hypocritical to pretend that I don't sympathise, but I do beg you not to go around expressing such sentiments to anyone else.'

75

'My dear, I wouldn't be such a fool. Although I don't suppose it makes a hoot of difference. Presumably, the police don't take the character and reputation of the victim into account as mitigating circumstances when they're dealing with murder, do they, Tessa?'

'No, I don't think they do. Did Alice have anything else to tell them?'

'As a matter of fact, she did, although it only came out as a sort of afterthought and I'm not sure how seriously one should take it. I don't think the Inspector was either. I imagine he thought, as I did, that she may have been making it up, to prove that she wasn't the last person to see Mrs Trelawney alive. She said that, as she was on the point of leaving yesterday, the front door bell rang. She assumed that it was the officer from the Council, whom she'd been warned about, but in fact it was a young woman who didn't look in the least like a Council worker. Needless to say, it gave her quite a turn.'

'So what then?'

'She tried to get rid of her, but she'd hardly started on that when Mrs Trelawney came downstairs and said she'd deal with it herself. So Alice went on her way and that was the last she saw of either of them.'

'Could she describe the young woman?'

'Only vaguely, but frankly I wouldn't have credited her with enough imagination to invent even that much, so per-haps after all it was true. Nice looking girl, she said, and well spoken, and she was wearing trousers, with something white on top.'

'I wouldn't call that very imaginative,' Elsa said. 'It is a description which would fit thousands of young women.'

'Millions,' I agreed, feeling thankful that I had put on a blue shirt that morning.

'Yes, but there was a little more to it than that. She said the girl hadn't been carrying any bag or brief case, which was one reason why she automatically rejected the idea that she came from the Council, and also that she was wearing a big, flashy ring with a blue stone in it.'

I had been afraid of that and, having already placed my hands under the table, I now gave the ring a half twist, so that it was palm side down.

'Very mysterious, if it's true, don't you agree?' Louise continued. 'Just turning up like that out of the blue! No car, no bicycle . . . at least . . . that is. . . .'

For the first time the light of triumph and excitement seemed to fade from her eyes and she tailed off, looking embarrassed and uncomfortable.

'That is, what?' Elsa asked her.

'Well, it so happens that there was a car parked not far off when she came out and, naturally, she took it that it belonged to this girl, but almost at once it moved off and by the time she got to the corner it was out of sight; so I don't suppose there was any connection really; just one more coincidence. And you can understand why the Inspector was looking dubious, by this time, although he didn't manage to shake her on any part of her story.'

'I should have expected him to look more than just dubious,' Elsa said. 'Personally, I never heard anything so improbable in my life. If this young woman really exists and really called at the house yesterday, on foot and dressed in that way, then she must belong round here, in which case surely Alice would have recognised her?'

I must have been quite as eager as she was to hear the answer to this one, but it did not provide much cheer.

Louise said, 'And that's another curious thing. Naturally, the question was put to her in various forms and each time Alice said that she had definitely not recognised her, and yet at the same time, she had the feeling that she'd seen her somewhere before. The last thing the Inspector said before I left them to it was that he'd like her to keep thinking about it, and if she ever got the slightest inkling of where she might have seen this girl, either in the flesh or in a photograph, she was to let him know immediately.'

*

Realising that it would be foolhardy to rely on Alice's elusive memory remaining elusive for ever, and that therefore my arrest on charges of conspiracy to murder might be imminent, I toyed for a while with the idea of driving down to the police station to give myself up. It would have been the dignified way of handling it and the one to cause the least embarrassment to my hostess, but the snag was that I considered it unlikely that the Inspector would believe my story for a single minute, and I did not think that I should blame him. What it boiled down to was that I had met Mrs Trelawney on one previous occasion, in the rather too distant past, among a large crowd of people and on a different continent. As a result of which I had felt impelled to seek her out in her new surroundings and without invitation, or the slightest encouragement, practically to force my way into her house.

Of course, if the Inspector had then invited me to pull the other one, as I had no doubt he would, I could have gone on to explain that there had been more to it than this and that my primary object had been to discover what kind of woman lurked beneath the bombast and bullying and how best she could be persuaded, coerced or threatened into desisting from her ruination of the countryside and the lives of its inhabitants. The trouble there was that I could not see how this was to be done without naming Elsa, among others, as my source of information, thereby setting her up as a potential murder suspect too.

I became so engrossed in this problem that it was some while before I noticed that Elsa was also looking distinctly preoccupied and depressed. There was no trace of that muted rejoicing one might have expected to find on the face of a woman, the bane and scourge of whose life had just been permanently removed, at no trouble or expense to herself, and it occurred to me that she was probably not thinking along such selfish lines at all, but was merely saddened by the thought that it had come about too late to save Geoffrey from his fatal heart attack. However, it presently emerged

that much more mundane considerations had been exercis-
ing her mind and that she was concerned with nothing more
profound than Toby's lunch.

'It would have done all right for us two,' she explained,
having gone into details about the shepherd's pie and stewed
apricots, 'but I'm not sure that I'd dare offer it to him. I think
I had better just nip in to Storhampton and get a few
avocados and things, to jolly it up a bit. It will mean making
lunch rather late, but I don't suppose he'll mind that, so long
as it's worth eating when he gets it.'

'Can't I go for you?' I asked, keeping my fingers crossed,
for I had now decided that, as an interim measure, my safest
bet was to skulk for as long as possible in the house and
grounds and not to tempt providence by blazoning myself
abroad, with the ever present risk of coming face to face with
Alice. Luckily, Elsa's response was all that I could have
wished for.

'No, I don't think that would do, thank you, Tessa, because
I shan't know what to get until I see it. You stay here and
entertain Toby till I get back.'

Nothing could have suited me better because, second only
to the right conditions for skulking, what I most needed in
this crisis in my life was a detached view of it from an outside
observer and it has sometimes been said that the world holds
few outsiders with more detached views on any subject you
care to name than my cousin Toby.

'It sounds to me,' he said, living up to this reputation, as we
strolled in the rose garden, 'as though my advice would be of
very little use to you. What you need now is a clever lawyer.'

'You really think it's as bad as that?'

'Not really, no. There is usually a way out. If they do come
and get you, I should simply deny everything.'

'That was my first thought, naturally, but I soon saw that it
would only get me into worse trouble. Dozens of people
could testify that I was wearing slacks and a white top
yesterday and also that I do possess a rather flamboyant
turquoise ring.'

79

'Then I suppose you will have to humble yourself and ask Robin's advice. I can quite understand your reluctance to admit that your meddling has landed you in quite a nasty pickle, but I am afraid this is pride swallowing time. He knows far more about these matters than you or I, or should do, by now.'

'I suppose you're right.'

'In any case, I have to confess that I have now rather lost interest in the whole affair. How tame and predictable it has turned out to be, and after such a promising start! A lot of people wishing to murder a tiresome old woman and eventually one of them does so. That's not much of a plot.'

'It is one which has been used in numerous successful plays, however. And, besides, you have over-simplified it. There are any number of sub-plots and cross currents threading their way in and out.'

'Well, that's cheering, I suppose. You had better tell me what they are. Be brief, though!'

'I shall start with the purloined camera,' I told him, 'and the photograph too few.'

Having done so, I added: 'And those are not the only puzzles which confront us.'

'That's good! What else?'

'Well, you see, the minute Millie told me that our local editor had turned us down, I detected the hand of Mrs Trelawney pulling strings in the background and, as a result of what you would no doubt call meddling, I had actually discovered, as I thought, how she had got wind of what we were up to. However, I was wrong.'

'It can happen to the best of us.'

'And a pardonable mistake, I maintain, in this case. When I heard that the young woman having tea in Mrs Parkinson's shop when Diane brought the camera in was the daughter of a woman who worked for Mrs Trelawney, I immediately concluded that the leak had come from her. Wouldn't you have done the same?'

'Yes, I expect so. Why were we both wrong?'

'The theory was shaken a bit as soon as I met Alice Hawkins, because she did not strike me as the type of woman who would be on gossipy terms with her employer. She seemed timid and unassertive, whereas Mrs Trelawney was a great big rumbustious bully and, in fact, it's my belief that if news had reached Alice that someone was about to spike those guns, far from interfering, she would have given it a round of applause.'

'You can't always tell, you know. It could be the Uriah Heep brand of timidity, compulsive favour currying.'

'The real crunch was her not having recognised me. That can't have been out of any noble ambition to go to the gallows in my place because she was so hell bent in getting herself out of the noose that she would cheerfully have thrown anyone to the lions at that point. So it must have been true.'

Noticing Toby's smug, amused expression, I went on, 'Kindly get it through your head that I don't expect to be recognised wherever I show my face, or have to fight off the clamouring fans, but if her daughter and son-in-law had really been talking to her about me so recently and, if, as a result, she'd known I was staying here with Elsa, then isn't it almost inconceivable that she wouldn't have made the connection when I turned up at Pettits Farm?'

'So you now believe that she hadn't heard a word about the photographs and that someone else passed on the information?'

'I honestly don't know what I believe any more. Perhaps the answer is simply that the editor cancelled our appointment for the reason he gave, or because he had second thoughts and got cold feet. They keep it very bland, you know, these local newspapers; never take sides, especially when the rich and powerful are involved. I ought to have taken that into account. Not that anything's lost, now that the old harridan is dead.'

'So what are you worried about? Apart from being arrested for her murder, of course?'

'Well, I'd still love to know what became of that missing photograph. It's even harder now to guess who might have taken it, and for what purpose.'

'I don't know why you keep harping on that. I expect Millie took it herself and then tried to put the blame on Diane, hoping to get her into trouble.'

'Oh, do you really think so?' I asked doubtfully. 'I know she hates Diane and is probably passionately jealous of her, but I don't think she'd stoop to anything so underhand as that.'

'No? How about the letter Diane gave her? Didn't you tell me that Millie was all for steaming it open?'

'Oh no . . . that was just a joke,' I said, more doubtfully than ever.

'Well, don't fail to let me know if anything a little more sensational than a missing photograph turns up. I should think our avocados must be about ready by now, wouldn't you?'

He was in for a shock, however. Not only were they unready, but non-existent as well. Elsa tossed out some remark about having changed her mind and decided to start with tomato salad instead, but I happened to know that the refrigerator had been bursting with tomatoes when she set forth to Storhampton. The stewed apricots were unadorned too, not an almond or macaroon in sight, so it was hard to see exactly what purpose the expedition had served. The abstracted, faraway look, although less pronounced, also reappeared from time to time and, since I could neither nerve myself to take the plunge and call at the police station, nor admit to Robin that I had blown it completely, I went to bed that night with all my problems still unsolved and one fresh one to add to them.

FRIDAY P.M.

Marc arrived after tea on the following day and it was immediately apparent that Elsa had gone to the opposite extreme from boastfulness in describing him as presentable and not bad-looking, because the years had been much kinder to him than to his sister, transforming him into a real custom-built Prince Charming. He had been about seventeen when we last met, still awkward and overgrown and strangely out of proportion, with hands much too large and a head a size or two too small. Now all these flaws had been smoothed out, with everything fitting neatly into place and with the added bonus of pleasing manners and a radiant smile.

Watching these in action, I found it all the more regrettable that Diane should be so awful for in appearance no two young people could have complemented each other more beautifully. On the other hand, I at least felt encouraged to persist in my campaign to bolster Millie's self-esteem. Since she and Marcus were fundamentally so alike, in colouring, features and bone structure, there could no longer be much doubt that she too would be well on her way to the knock-out class the minute she stopped scowling and laid off the banana cake.

We were in the kitchen, as usual, when he arrived and inevitably the first hour or so was devoted almost exclusively to bringing him up to date with the stirring events of the past four days, with Elsa as principle narrator and Millie and me filling in whenever her breath or memory ran out.

She took it in chronological order and by the time she reached the climax Marc, whose eyes had been popping throughout, was as gratifyingly amazed, thunderstruck and attentive an audience as anyone could have wished for.

'Dead?' he repeated in an incredulous voice. 'You're not

83

pulling my leg? You honestly mean she's dead?'

'Oh yes.'

'I just can't believe it. Someone's actually had the guts at last to finish the old witch off! Well, good on 'em, eh?'

'Now, Marc, you really will have to be careful not to say things like that, you know,' Elsa told him reprovingly. 'All of us here realise it's a joke, but some people might not understand.'

'Don't you believe it,' he said, not in the least abashed. 'They'd understand perfectly, and I bet some of them are wishing they'd had the sense to do it months ago, seeing how simple it turns out to have been. I wonder who did do it, though, if the police are right in treating the burglary stunt as a fake? One of the estate workers who'd got it in for her, perhaps? Oh well, let's just hope they don't catch him, and I must go and ring up Diane this very minute and offer my congratulations. All right if I ask her over for a celebration dinner, Ma?'

'She's not there,' Millie said, with the merest hint of triumph in her voice.

'What do you mean not there, fathead? This is Friday, remember? She always makes a point of getting home by six on Friday when she knows I'm coming down.'

'Yes, only you see, darling . . .' Elsa began, but Millie was not to be denied.

'She's in Bexhill.'

'You're joking! What would she want to go there for?'

'To stay with an aunt. Her mother's had another turn and Diane has taken her for a little holiday by the sea.'

Marc looked angry and puzzled, then tried to cover his disappointment with a jauntiness which deceived none of us.

'Well, well, talk about absent-minded! Never a word of this to me!'

'It was all arranged in such a hurry, you see,' Elsa explained, getting her oar in at last. 'Cheer up, darling! She's only gone for a few days, so she might be back by tomorrow, or Sunday anyway. And what Millie didn't tell you is that

84

she's written you a note to explain all about it. It's upstairs in your bedroom.'

Marc left us without a word and, turning to Millie, Elsa said reproachfully, 'I do wish you wouldn't be so tactless! Why did you have to fling it at him like that?'

'Don't see what difference it'd have made if I'd handed it to him on a bed of watercress. She'd still be in Bexhill.'

'Yes, I know, but there are ways and ways of doing things and I don't think yours was very kind.'

'Oh, here we go again, blaming me for everything! Everything's always my fault. We don't hear much about Diane being unkind to go skipping off to Bexhill without bothering to let him know. Oh no, that would never enter your head, would it? You'd always find excuses for her! It's just stupid, boring old Millie who makes all the trouble and I'm getting bloody fed up with it, if you want to know.'

Her face had been turning scarlet during this plunge into self-pity and at the end of it, evidently finding this as good a curtain line as she was likely to hit on, she jumped up, crashed her chair against the table and fled from the room, slamming the door behind her.

'What a charming way to start the weekend!' Elsa commented bitterly, now looking close to tears herself.

'Yes, I'm afraid my so-called influence didn't go very deep. In fact, I may have done more harm than good by encouraging her to think well of herself. She was nicer when she didn't.'

'Oh no, it has nothing to do with you, it's almost always like this nowadays. And I look forward to it all the week, you know, the three of us being here together. Each time I vow that, whatever happens, I'll keep the peace, even if it means turning myself into a zombie, and each time Millie manages to break down my defences. Then I hear myself sounding like a prissy old maiden aunt and the next thing you know we're up to our necks in one of these scenes.'

'Take heart! She'll be back at school in a week or two.'

Elsa sighed. 'I'm afraid that's not going to help much. She'll still be at home at weekends and that's when all the trouble starts. She's not so bad when we're here on our own.'

The door opened and the subject of this lament stuck her head round it, to announce in defiant tones that she was going out to see someone called Janie and probably wouldn't be back for dinner.

'Oh, I see! Well, all right, darling, but try not to be too late, won't you? You know how I worry!'

'Oh, God!' Millie groaned, not forgetting to slam the door again.

Seeing how infuriating her last reminder must have been to any sensitive sixteen-year-old, I was wondering whether I dared point out to Elsa a few of the errors of her ways, when the door opened again and this time it was Marc who made the dramatic entrance. In fact, the whole evening was becoming more like a stage production every minute and I was quite sorry that Toby was not present to pick up a few tips, specially as Marc was able to provide us with something slightly more enthralling than a display of adolescent tantrums.

We could tell at once that something had gone seriously wrong in his life because all the self-confidence and buoyancy had oozed away, leaving him a little shrunk and beaten looking. He was holding Diane's letter, but his opening question concerned Millie.

'She's gone out,' Elsa told him.

'Well, that's one blessing, anyway! To have her crowing and trumpeting about might be a little more than I could stand just at this moment. Perhaps we can hush it up for a bit? Or does she know already, by any chance? Did everyone know except me?'

'Know what, darling?'

'About Diane?'

'Yes, of course she knew. What's the matter with you, Marc? She told you herself, just now, that Diane had gone to Bexhill.'

'I don't mean that. Bexhill was just an excuse.'

'I simply 'don't understand you, darling. An excuse for what? You mean she hasn't gone there at all? But. . . .'

'Oh, she's gone all right, but all that stuff about having to take her mother down there was just twaddle. She's gone because she couldn't face me. She was afraid I'd go straight up to Orchard House and make one hell of a scene and ask her what she thought she was up to. She's damn right too. That's exactly what I would have done.'

'I do wish you'd explain what this is all about,' Elsa said, showing a certain obtuseness, in my opinion, or perhaps not yet daring to believe the obvious, which Marc now proceeded to deliver in plain terms.

'She's chucked me over, that's what! Backed out, turned me down, called it off! Refused to marry me, if you prefer!'

'Oh, my dearest boy, how dreadful for you! What an awful thing to do, and how extraordinary! You hadn't quarrelled, had you?'

'No, Diane's like you, she never quarrels with anyone. You ought to know that by now.'

'Then why? What reason does she give? She hasn't . . . found someone else?'

'No, nothing like that. Her motives are of the purest and most disinterested. She says it wouldn't be fair to me for us to be married. She's thought about it a lot and in her heart she knows she's not really cut out to be the wife of someone as ambitious as I am, not clever enough to keep up and she'd only damage my career. Did you ever hear such rot?'

'Well, in a way . . . No, no, of course I didn't. I find it quite incomprehensible. What would any of that matter, if you really love each other?'

'She says it's because she really does love me that she's made up her mind to break it off. She's finally decided that she wants me to have my freedom. Not hers, mark you, mine!'

Presumably, Elsa and I were both wearing our sceptical expressions a little too openly by this time, because he said defensively:

'Okay, I know it sounds loony, and so it would be in anyone else, but Diane's like that. That's the way her mind works, and she's got this stupid, ridiculous sense of inferiority. And she does give another reason why it wouldn't be fair to me, quite a practical one this time, in case you're interested?'

'You know very well that I am.'

'She says that, with this move coming up and nothing whatever settled about where they're to go, it might be ages before we could actually get married, and I suppose you have to admit that's realistic. Neither of her parents is capable of organising anything at all in that way. They'd get themselves into one hell of a muddle, financially as well as every other way, so it'll fall to Diane to arrange everything and she could hardly do that, if she was living with me in London.'

'Yes, I do see that, but it won't take forever. You'd be perfectly prepared to wait for another few months, I imagine?'

Marc hesitated and a gleam of what looked suspiciously like guilty amusement momentarily lightened his expression. 'Well, yes, of course . . . but you know . . . it wouldn't be easy. It hasn't always been easy in the past. Oh well, I'll just have to wait until she gets back and then see how long she can stand out against my fatal charm. It might mean staying on here for a couple of days, if that's all right with you, Ma? In the meantime, I think I'll go down to the pub and drown by sorrows. I take it the car's in running order now?'

'Oh yes, all fixed up now, but do be careful, won't you? Driving back, I mean.'

'Oh, for God's sake!' he exploded, sounding exactly like Millie. 'I'm only going to have a game of darts and a pint of lager.'

'From which I deduce that with Diane it's ring first and bed later?' I suggested, when Marc had gone.

'Yes, I'm afraid so. I've always suspected that she was rather a cold little fish underneath all the gush. I used to be quite pleased about that at one time. I thought Marc would grow tired of being dangled on a string and would turn to someone a little more earthy, but I was quite wrong. Being unattainable only seems to have enhanced those charms. I wonder what her game is now, though?'

'You take it for granted there is one?'

'Yes, I'm sorry to say I do.'

'No chance that she's such a frigid fish that when it's getting close to the crunch she can't face marriage at all?'

'It could be, I suppose, and I may be doing her a grave injustice, but I have a feeling, in that case, it would be the ring first and the chronic headache ever after. No, what I'm really afraid is that her aim now is to plunge him into even lower depths of slavish love, so as to give the screws an extra turn.'

'To what end?'

'Well, it's perfectly true that it would be difficult for her to get married and leave her family in the lurch, so long as they have this eviction order hanging over them, so I suppose this was an attempt to force Marc into taking some action.'

'Like murdering the landlady, for instance, if he hadn't been forestalled in the meantime?'

'Now, now, Tessa dear, don't be silly! You know perfectly well that I didn't mean anything of the kind.'

'Then what kind of thing did you mean?'

'Well, so far with Marc, one must admit that it's been a lot of wild threats and hot air and nothing much else, and I expect Diane got it into her head that, with his legal training and such small influence as our family has in these parts, he could perhaps have been a little more constructive; made some direct approach, say to David Trelawney. I daresay she reckoned that, if it was a question of his losing her or taking up the cudgels, he wouldn't hesitate for a second. Judging by his reaction this evening, I am bound to say that she was probably right. Of course, the situation has changed now and it may no longer be necessary for Marc or anyone else to intervene, but I'm sure that's what was in her mind.'

'So, as things have turned out, you may still be stuck with

her, despite her noble renunciation? Oh well, let's not be too pessimistic. When Marc's had time to cool off, he may well see this for what it is, a bit of cheap blackmail; and then perhaps the scales will fall from his eyes. I'd say there was a fair chance of that and, whatever else, Mrs Trelawney won't be around to harass you any more. So let's follow the advice Millie's always giving us and Think Positive, while we have the chance.'

The chance was not to be ours for long, however, for it was scarcely half an hour later that, much to my horror and annoyance, we received a visitor in the person of Inspector Bledlow of the Dedley C.I.D. He appeared to have little interest in me, however, and I was subjected to nothing more daunting than a sharp, appraising look when he learnt my identity. It was Marcus he had really come to see and, on hearing this, Elsa promptly collapsed in a dead faint.

'She is recovering from a nasty bout of flu,' I explained re-entering the room a few minutes later, with the brandy bottle in one hand and a glass of water in the other, 'and a close friend has just died very suddenly, so the smallest shock is liable to unnerve her.'

Elsa was now sitting up, although still pale and distraught looking. She accepted the glass of water and sipped it very slowly, presumably to give herself a little time to think, in the event of the Inspector finding my explanation inadequate to account for her passing out at the mention of her son's name.

Perhaps he did not, though, because he said mildly, 'I am sorry to hear that and very sorry indeed to be the cause of further distress, but, as I told you, my business is really with Mr Marcus Carrington and I was told that I might find him here this evening. Is he at home, by any chance?'

He was altogether a reassuringly mild looking man, although not lacking in authority. I judged him to be about fifty, and he was below average in height and on the burly side, with a round head and crinkly brown hair. There were a lot of crinkles round his eyes too and deep horizontal lines on his forehead, which suggested that smiling came naturally to him, although he was not doing any now.

'Not here just at the moment,' I replied, since Elsa still seemed incapable of speech, 'He's gone to ... see some friends, but he'll be back soon, I expect. Can I give him a message?'

'What time do you expect him, then?'

'I'm not sure. Around nine, wouldn't you say, Elsa?'

She nodded. 'About then.'

The Inspector, who had not taken his eyes off her, even while ostensibly speaking to me, was looking thoughtful.

'I see. Well, if he should be back any earlier, would you be kind enough to ask him to give me a ring? The number's on this card and I'll be in my office till eight-thirty or so. Failing that, first thing in the morning?'

'Yes, of course.'

'It's quite important,' he added, moving to the door. 'Don't get up, either of you, I'll see myself out.'

I thought he must then have broken into a sprint because we heard the sound of a car engine seconds before he should, by rights, have reached the front door. Unfortunately, it was the wrong car and two minutes later he was back.

'Your son has just returned, Mrs Carrington and I've asked him to accompany me to the station. Just a small matter I want to clear up and it shouldn't take long. Very sorry to have disturbed you. Good evening!'

'What do you suppose that's all about?' I asked.

'I don't have to suppose anything. I know only too well what it's about.'

'Oh, really? Is that why you were looking so worried yesterday?'

'Yes, I was so desperately afraid something like this would happen, and now it has, you see!'

'You've left me far behind, Elsa, because today you'd stopped looking so worried and yet, as you correctly point out, now it has happened.'

'And just when I was beginning to feel safe, when I'd managed to convince myself that there was nothing in it and the scare was all of my own making. I might have guessed that they'd wait till this evening, when they knew Marc would be here. Although I suppose you could take that as a moderately good sign, couldn't you?'

'A good sign of what?'

'That they didn't regard it as so urgent that they had to go chasing up to London to see him; that twenty-four hours, one way or the other, wouldn't make much difference?'

'Honestly, Elsa, I'm doing my best, but since you're the only one of us who knows what you're talking about, I do find it a little hard to give you the advice and reassurance you are obviously craving for.'

'Yes, I'm sorry, Tessa, but I haven't quite got myself together yet. It's about Marc's car, you see!'

'Oh yes?'

'Well, he leaves it down here during the week. He couldn't really use it much in London and garaging is so expensive, so it makes sense.'

'And he goes back and forth to London by train?'

'Yes, I always take him to the station on Monday and, if I know what train he'll be on, I usually try to meet him. If not, he gets a taxi up here, as he did this evening.'

'I think I've grasped all that, but why should it interest Inspector Bledlow?'

'If you'll cast your mind back to last Wednesday, the day before yesterday, I'll tell you exactly why. The house, as you may remember, was deserted for at least two hours, from about three o'clock onwards. I had my Darby and Joan party and Millie was playing at revolutionaries with her friends in Dedley; and you . . . I can't remember exactly what you were up to, but, being the model guest, you told me that you'd spent the afternoon relaxing in the fresh air.'

'Yes, that more or less describes it. And so?'

'After we'd finished our good works I drove Louise home.

Tim was using their car to take the poor dog down to the vet to be destroyed, which he'd promised to see to while she was out, so naturally I'd offered her a lift. When we turned off the Dedley road into her lane there was a little red sports car driving along about a hundred yards ahead of us, too far off to read the number plate, but, without any prompting, we both assumed it was Marc's. It went past the Macadams and on towards Orchard House.'

'Where it stopped?'

'I don't know. We'd lost sight of it by then, but I assumed that it was Marc and that he'd gone to see Diane. I felt a little cross with him, because this is the last run-up to his exams, but not all that surprised, you know. It wouldn't have been the first time he'd done such a thing and I was sure that when I got home I'd find a note from him saying that he was planning to spend the night here. All the same, I was puzzled.'

'Why?'

'Well, because it was only about five o'clock, which seemed to indicate that he knew she'd taken a few days off from work, otherwise she wouldn't have been home by then; yet on the other hand he obviously didn't know that she'd taken her mother to Bexhill. That didn't make sense, so then I told myself that we'd been mistaken and that it wasn't Marc's car, after all, and for the time being that was that.'

'But not for long?'

'No. Louise invited me in for a cup of tea, which I was dying for, and I spent about an hour with her. We were talking mainly about poor old Geoffrey, who'd died that morning. When I got home Marc's car was in the garage, looking exactly as it had when I went out in the morning. In a sort of superstitious way, I put my hand on the bonnet, and it was only just faintly warm, as you'd expect, with the sun streaming in all the afternoon, and there was no message when I went indoors. So that was the end of it, until yesterday morning.'

'When Louise came round to tell us that Mrs Trélawney

had been murdered on Wednesday afternoon?'

'Exactly! Do you remember how her manner changed when she mentioned the car which Alice had seen driving away when she was shutting the gate? Quite suddenly and for no apparent reason, she became evasive, almost guilty-looking, or so it seemed to me. Otherwise, I'm sure I wouldn't have read anything sinister into it, certainly not made the connection, but after she'd gone I became steadily more convinced that the car had been Marc's, or twin brother to it. I couldn't stop thinking about it. It kept going round and round in my head and then coming back to the starting point again and finally I was in such a state that I had to find out for certain, however bad it might be. I had to know where Marc had been and what he was doing on Wednesday afternoon. Only it was going to be tricky and I'd have to be careful how I put it, maybe tell a few lies even, and that meant that I couldn't do it where you might over-hear me. So I made an excuse to go down to the village and I rang him from the post office.'

'I see! So that's why we didn't get our avocados? How did you put it, incidentally?'

'That was pure inspiration, which hit me on the way down. I felt terribly ashamed of myself for being so devious, but I think you'll agree that it was rather subtle. I told him that I'd tried to move his car out of the garage that morning, to get at something which was stored at the back, but that I hadn't been able to do so because the battery was flat, and so what did he want me to do about it? I thought I'd be able to tell immediately from his reaction whether or not he'd been driving it himself on the previous afternoon.'

'Clever, indeed! And what was his reaction?'

'Everything I could have wished for. He didn't sound wildly surprised, just faintly irritated, as one would be in the circumstances, but taking it in his stride, and he asked me to get the garage to send someone up to have it put on charge. Fortunately, he didn't specify which garage and I thought, if any questions were to arise about that later on, I'd simply say that he wasn't to worry and that I'd had it put on my account.'

'And that was all there was to it?'

'On that subject, yes, but I wanted to keep everything as normal as possible, so I asked him what train he'd be coming by this evening and he said that it depended on how the work went and that he'd take a taxi up. Oh, and he sent you his love and said he was looking forward to seeing you and I'm sorry I wasn't able to pass that message on. I took it as almost the best sign of all, though; the fact that he was able to give his mind to ordinary things and speak of them so naturally and cheerfully, which I felt sure wouldn't have been the case if he'd been concealing anything. I don't mind telling you, Tessa, that when I walked out of the post office and drove back here I was feeling ten years younger.'

'You looked it too!'

'Not any more, though. Not after what's happened now.'

'So now you think perhaps he was concealing something, after all, and putting on a very convincing act?'

'No, I do not, not for one minute. I know Marc better than that and, for one thing, he's much too impulsive to carry it off. He speaks first and thinks later. That's one reason why he hasn't made himself very popular in certain quarters.'

'You said something like that once before. What are the other reasons?'

'Oh, some of them find him arrogant and conceited. It's not true, of course. He's really quite modest and shy underneath all that sort of swagger he sometimes puts on in public, but so few people bother to look below the surface, do they? He also has rather a quirky sense of humour, which sometimes gets him into trouble.'

'Oh really? What form does that take?'

'Practical jokes. It's something he inherited, or maybe copied from his father and I must confess that I don't find them awfully funny. In fact, they're apt to be quite cruel and humiliating, which is strange when you consider how sensitive he is in other ways. But I've never been able to make him

95

understand how objectionable some people find it. He once played a particularly unkind one on the Macadams. It wasn't long before their only child was run over and killed, which seemed to make it worse, in a curious way, and I know Louise has never entirely forgiven him. She wouldn't admit it to me, but . . . Oh, Louise! Oh, how can I have been so blind?'

'About Louise?'

'Yes. All the time I've been talking to you, even when the Inspector was here, there's been a question hovering at the back of my mind.'

'Mine too, several in fact. How does Louise answer yours?'

'The question was, you see, even if it had been a car just like Marc's which Alice saw, how would she have recognised it as such? It's not as though she'd ever worked here, or knew us at all well, so it's really most unlikely. But I was simple, wasn't I? I see now that what must have happened was that Louise told the Inspector about the one she and I saw and how we'd both assumed it was Marc driving it and when the description matched the one Alice had seen he put two and two together. It's hard to believe that an old friend could be so treacherous, but really it's the only way to account for all that evasiveness and embarrassment on her part.'

'No, it isn't, you're jumping much too far ahead. It's much more likely that Alice gave a rough description, which could have fitted dozens of cars besides Marc's, but was close enough to make Louise veer away from the subject when she was reporting to you. It doesn't follow that she added any-thing off her own bat.'

'I only hope you're right. It's not very nice to think of her doing anything so mean.'

'Actually, though, from Marc's point of view,' I remarked thoughtfully, 'it might be better if I were wrong.'

'Now why do you say that?'

'Well, listen, Elsa, we have to face the fact that if you and Louise, and most likely Alice too, saw that car at some point during the afternoon, then almost inevitably other people did, as well. You said it was too far off for you to read the number plate and it's a safe bet that Alice didn't even try to. There was no reason to. Therefore, if Louise had been the one to pass on the news, it would have proved nothing. I'm very much afraid, in view of their present approach, that the police must have found someone who got a much closer view of it, perhaps in the vicinity of Pettits Farm and who either noticed the registration number and were able to recall it later, or else identified it positively as Marc's.'

'Do you realise what you're saying, Tessa? Would you, by any remote chance, be suggesting that Marc would have lied to me?'

'He didn't actually need to, did he? You didn't put the direct question concerning his whereabouts on Wednesday afternoon.'

'Well, perhaps not in so many words, but he allowed me to believe that he was in London, which amounts to the same thing.'

I was not so sure that it did, but knew we should get nowhere, if a breath of criticism were to be blown on the beamish boy, so I skipped over this point by saying, 'In that case, we should consider the alternatives.'

'What are they?'

'On the premise that it was his car and that there exists at least one reliable witness to confirm it, we can only conclude that someone else was driving it, which raises a couple more questions. First of all, is the Darby and Joan party a regular occurrence?'

'Yes, we hold it on the last Wednesday of every month.'

'And you always attend?'

'Except in very rare circumstances, yes, always.'

'Do most people round here know that?'

'Oh, I'm sure they all do. Quite a lot of other women, and a few men too, help out from time to time, including poor old Geoffrey, although even he couldn't induce Millie to give us a hand. Anyway, Louise and I are the mainstays and we hardly ever miss. I see what you're getting at, Tessa, and I must say I think it's very bright of you.'

'Because, of course, the anti-nuclear rally would also have been well publicised in advance, so that took care of Millie, whereas my being here was something which no one could have forseen.'

'Yes, you're right, it does begin to make sense, although it's almost inconceivable that anyone we know could have done such a thing.'

'Which brings us to the second question. How many sets of keys are there?'

'Marc has his own, of course. I have one.'

'And Marc takes his to London with him?'

'Sometimes. Sometimes he just leaves them in the pocket of whatever he happened to be wearing.'

'And what about your set? Do you carry it around in your bag, for instance?'

'Yes, usually, but there's no rule about it. Quite often they're left lying on the hall table, which is where they are now, as a matter of fact. I sometimes use the car myself, you see, when mine is being serviced or lets me down for some reason. Marc is all in favour of it. Much better for it to have a little exercise from time to time.'

'And those are the only two sets?'

'Well, no, there is a third, as it happens, a kind of emergency set, Marc and I both being compulsive mislayers of essential articles. It used to be kept in a drawer in my desk, along with the log book and insurance certificate.'

'Used to be, but not any more?'

'Curiously enough, I think Diane may have it.'

'Oh, not that old Diane creeping up on us again?'

'I could be wrong, but I think that's where it must be. She got round Marc to give her some driving lessons, you see, and she used to practice things like turning and so on in the drive, which is a lot more than he'd let anyone else do, including Millie, I might add, but of course he's practically besotted about that girl, poor darling, and you may be sure she made it plain that she couldn't afford lessons from a professional. It must be over a week now since I first noticed that those spare keys weren't in their usual place, and I've been meaning to ask him about it. Unfortunately, it's the kind of thing I only remember when he's not here.'

'He might have left them in a pocket, I suppose?'

'Not that set, no. He keeps special clothes for wearing down here and they're usually left lying in a heap on the floor on Monday morning. I always go through the pockets because he's quite capable of leaving his cheque book and God knows what else in them. He's so utterly careless about possessions.'

'Whereas Diane, as we know, has rather the opposite sort of weakness; not above absent-mindedly popping other people's belongings into her shopping bag.'

'All the same, it can't have been Diane who was using the car on Wednesday. For one thing, she hasn't passed her test yet and, for another, she was already in Bexhill.'

'It might be as well to make sure of that?'

'I am sure. Marigold was helping out at the Darby and Joan, so naturally I asked her whether her mother had got off all right and she said yes, and that the aunt had telephoned just after lunch to say that they'd both arrived and everything seemed to be going splendidly.'

'Oh well, Diane could have passed the keys on to someone else. She may even have left them in Mrs Parkinson's shop. One way and another, they could be pretty well anywhere by now, which personally I regard as very good news.'

'Is it? I'm afraid I'm not thinking very clearly. The only news that would give me any pleasure just now would be for Marc to walk in and say it was all a mistake, some stupid misunderstanding and nothing whatever to do with Mrs Trelawney's murder.'

Curiously enough, when he did walk in, which happened about half an hour later, this was very much in line with the tale he had to relate. Unfortunately, however, far from putting an end to the business, the explanation only succeeded in tangling it up still further.

*

'The most idiotic and ridiculous muddle,' he told us, sounding quite cheerful about it and helping himself to a drink. 'I simply couldn't imagine what the fellow was driving at and I still can't. Honestly, if this is the state the law has got into, I think it's high time I switched to another profession.'

'What was it all about, then? What did he want?' Elsa asked, starting to look ten years younger again, although she still had several more to lose before re-entering her true age group.

'I tell you, I never properly discovered what it was all about. Some parking offence, presumably, or speeding in a thirty mile limit. Anyway, he'd got hold of completely the wrong end of the stick and when I'd told him so about four times I think it sank in.'

'But, darling, why should he drag you down to the station for a trivial thing like that?'

'Precisely what I asked myself. An Inspector, mark you! Complete with sergeant in attendance, to take down my statement! Naturally, at the start, I thought it must be something quite different they were after and all the questions about the car were just a cover-up, some elaborate kind of trap, but apparently not. At the end of it all he seemed quite satisfied. Said something about how he'd need to check one or two points, but didn't think it would be necessary to see me again. I should hope not, indeed! After that, the sergeant drove me home and here I am!'

'And I'm delighted to see you. I'll get something done about the dinner in a minute, because I'm sure you must be starving, but I do wish you'd tell me a little more about this strange affair. What kind of questions did the Inspector ask you?'

'Only two was what it amounted to, but he kept putting them in different languages, so that one had the illusion there were dozens. What it actually boiled down to was where my car had been on Wednesday afternoon.'

'So what did you tell him?'

'Oh, Ma, how you do go on, don't you? Naturally, I told

him that it had been tucked up in its little garage because I only use it at weekends and I'd spent the whole of last Wednesday in London.'

'Did he want you to prove it?'

'He seemed to think it would be a nice idea, but unfortunately I was unable to oblige. I've been flat out on all this blasted revision and one day has been pretty much like another. I can't even remember whether anyone telephoned me on Wednesday; might not have noticed if they had. Pretty feeble, isn't it? I'm sure Tessa would have come up with something much more convincing, but since I hadn't the remotest idea what they were on about, it didn't seem worth while inventing any fancy lies.'

'Oh, that would have been my advice, too,' I assured him. 'Fancy lies can get people into no end of trouble. I hope you stuck to the same principle when he was asking you about the car?'

'Yes, indeed! And of course I was on firmer ground there, wasn't I?'

'Were you?' Elsa asked faintly. 'Why was that?'

'Simply because I was able to say without fear or fumble that it had never left the garage, having been reliably informed by my mother, who has never once been known to deviate from the truth in her entire life, that at daybreak on Thursday the battery was as dead as a doornail. How then could it have been taken out, by her or anyone else, not much more than twelve hours earlier? I'd probably left the lights on, or something equally daft, when I was down last weekend, but batteries don't go flat overnight all by themselves in this weather. It's okay, Ma! No need to look so doom laden! I'm sure I got it through to him in the end. Probably the worst that can happen is that he'll be after you to confirm all this, but that shouldn't present any problem.'

SATURDAY A.M.

'So this is your great crime prevention excercise?' Robin asked the following morning, 'Forgive my saying that I don't think much of it. Judging by what has been going on here during the past five days, I would hate to see what happened when you were trying to incite a crime.'

Making the most of a rare Saturday off duty, he had arrived at Pettits Grange soon after breakfast and I had barely allowed him more time than to say hallo to his hostess, before dragging him off for a stroll in the woods, a proposal which had received the warmest encouragement from Elsa, who indeed had been the one to suggest it. She had come into my room when I was getting ready to go to bed the night before and had impressed upon me that she was now relying on Robin to extricate herself and Marc from the mess her well meaning efforts had got them into, and that the first move should be to acquaint him with past events and the prospect of further upheavals ahead.

'I hardly see how you can blame me for any of it,' I said in answer to his accusations. 'If there'd been more time, things might have worked out differently, but since Mrs Trelawney was killed two days after I arrived here, there was really nothing much I could have done to prevent it. It begins to look as though the crime was planned down to the last detail before I made my unexpected appearance. In fact, my being here at all and, in particular, my calling on her that very afternoon might seriously have upset matters, if the timing had been only very slightly different. To that extent, you could say that I only failed to avert a murder by a matter of minutes.'

'Or failed to make it a double murder by exactly the same margin.'

'Yes, I hadn't thought of that. So perhaps it was all for the best! Incidentally, Robin, it's not very flattering to my vanity, but I suppose I should also be grateful for the fact that Alice still hasn't the faintest idea who I am, so at least I don't have that to worry about.'

'I wouldn't be too sure of it, if I were you.'

'Oh, but it's days ago now. If no bell has rung yet, I must be pretty safe.'

'It may not have been Alice who reported that you were wandering about near Pettits Farm that afternoon, but some-one sent Bledlow an anonymous letter about it.'

'Really? How do you know? Why haven't you told me this before?'

'Haven't had much chance really, have I?'

'But how do you know?'

'From the horse's mouth. He rang me up and told me.'

'Why? Is he a friend of yours?'

'Not really. He came here a year or two after I was moved on, but we've met once or twice since then and a lot of people in the Force know that you're my wife, or perhaps I should say that I'm your husband. He thought I might be interested.'

'Just that?'

'Well no, there was a little more. He was quite keen to know whether Anon had got his facts right.'

'And what did you reply to that?'

'That he most likely had; that you were staying here with friends and that, being a great walker, it was not unusual to find you padding about the countryside on a summer afternoon.'

'And that was all?'

'Not quite. Naturally, it occurred to him to ask whether you had ever met the deceased, to which I replied with a categorical no. I see now that I was a bit hasty there. It does rather alter the situation.'

'I don't see why. Our previous acquaintance had certainly not set up any desire to murder her, should the chance arise some time in the future. In fact, she was exceptionally civil and hospitable on that first occasion. Probably felt she was queen of her own patch, instead of an outcast in hoity-toity Sowerley, which I take to have been at the root of her disgusting conduct.'

'The trouble is that I inadvertently led Bledlow to believe that it was entirely out of the question that you had ever set eyes on her, far less that you could have been with her in the very room where she was found dead so soon afterwards. I honestly think it might be the decent thing for you and me to pay a call on him some time this morning.'

'Oh, very well, if you insist, although there's nothing I can tell him that he won't already have heard from Alice. In the meantime, what about Elsa?'

'What about her?'

'Will he want her to confirm Marc's story about the car and, if so, what line should she take?'

'She hasn't much choice, has she? He'll probably begin by asking her quite casually and gently, whether it was true about the battery and, if she says yes, indeed, he'll appear to be quite satisfied and to take her word for it. Then, when she's breathing out great gusty sighs of relief and beginning to let her guard down, he'll say that, purely as a matter of routine, he'll have to ask her to supply the name of the garage who fixed it. And then what?'

'Would he really be so mean?'

'What's mean about it? If she's lied to him, he has every right to make things awkward for her. My advice would be to own up before it gets to that.'

'How can she, though, without making things awkward for Marc? She would have to explain why she went to such lengths to find out tactfully whether he had been driving around here on Wednesday afternoon and that would inevitably lead to explaining that both she and Louise had instantly taken it for granted that it was his car they saw and that her anxiety sprang from the fact that he had personally threatened to kill Mrs Trelawney.'

'I daresay he'll have heard that from numerous sources

already, since you tell me that he didn't confine these proud boasts to the family circle. So she won't do him much good by trying to conceal anything there. Quite the reverse, in fact. If the boy's own mother took these threats so seriously, why should Bledlow be expected to laugh them off?'

'So she's in a jam, whichever way she plays it?'

'Not necessarily. There are still those missing keys to be accounted for and he'll be much more likely to believe her there, if she's been honest with him about the other thing.'

'He wouldn't just assume that she'd buried them in the garden, or that they never existed?'

'That might occur to him, but on the other hand, there must be no end of people to confirm that they did exist and also that she was pretty free about lending them out. It would at least give him something to work on. I don't think there's much point in trying to kid ourselves that it wasn't Marc's car, so the only question is: was he driving it, or was someone else? If the second, it would have to be someone who knew his way around the house and, presumably, also someone who had sufficient grudge against young Mr Carrington not to feel squeamish about landing him in a sea of trouble. That ought to narrow the field a little.'

'No as much as you might suppose. Elsa is quite the most trusting woman who ever lived and to describe her as keeping open house is the literal truth. She hardly ever locks any doors, even at night, and people seem to wander in and out whenever they feel like it. Furthermore, she has told me on two occasions that Marc has managed to make quite a few enemies around here.'

'All the more reason for supposing that one of them had felt vengeful enough to play such a vindictive trick.'

'Of course, it may all be sheer coincidence. Someone could have borrowed the car for quite an innocent purpose. It doesn't absolutely follow that whoever it was also killed Mrs Trelawney.'

'I think it almost does. However well known Elsa's reputation for casualness about her premises and property, I find it hard to imagine anyone with perfectly innocent motives calmly walking in, picking up the keys and driving off in one of her cars, without some sort of by-your-leave, or at the very least confessing to it afterwards, and returning the keys at the same time, incidentally. At any rate, I still think this is her best, if not her only chance of getting Marc off Bledlow's hook.'

'In which case, we ought to hurry back right now and out-line the script to her.'

'I am only afraid that he may have forestalled us.'

'Not too much danger of that because the minute we left she planned to bolt down to Storhampton and conceal her-self in a supermarket. She often goes early on Saturday morning, to stock up for the weekend, so Marc won't find anything unusual about it and she means to spin it out, to make sure we're back before she is.'

'I love the way you lay on all these amusing weekend recreations,' Robin said, brushing off the dust and chips of bark which had stuck to his trousers. 'They always make such a pleasant change from the dull routine of work.'

Elsa had not returned, but there was an unfamiliar car parked behind Robin's, some distance from the front door. However, as it was a very dashing Mercedes, almost split new, neither of us was inclined to associate it with Inspector Bledlow. The owner, we concluded, was the fair haired young man standing with his back to us under the porch.

He turned round as we approached, either hearing our feet crunching on the gravel, or perhaps because he had been on the point of leaving anyway, for, advancing towards us with a sunny smile, he said, 'Out of luck, I'm afraid. There doesn't appear to be anyone at home.'

Seeing him thus, at close quarters, I could understand the doubts that had been expressed concerning his qualifications for the job of farm manager, and also why it had been grudgingly conceded that he was not bad looking and had pleasant enough manners.

He was slightly built, four or five inches shorter than Robin, with very small hands and feet and his face, too, was small and doll-like. There was something almost babyish looking about him and it was impossible to imagine him ever maturing into middle age.

'And those that are, still in bed, I wouldn't wonder,' I told him. 'Is there anything we can do? I'm Theresa Price, by the way, and this is Robin, my husband. We're staying here.'

'David Trelawney, how do you do?' he replied, shaking hands.

'How do you do? Who did you want to see?'

'Well, Mrs Carrington, actually, if she'd been able to spare me a few minutes.'

'Oh, I'm sorry, she's gone shopping. Would you like to come in and wait, or shall we give her a message?'

'If you'd just tell her I called? It's a personal matter I wanted to see her about. Well, that's to say, not exactly personal, but confidential.'

'Oh, I see! Well, she's sure to be back quite soon. Why not come in?'

I was hoping he would agree to this, being keen to further the acquaintance, but evidently the desire was not reciprocated because, looking rather bashful and awkward, as though fearful of giving offence, he said, 'Well . . . er . . . most awfully kind of you . . . but perhaps not, thanks ever so much . . . everything's rather difficult at the moment. . . .'

'Yes, we did hear. I'm so sorry.'

'Thanks. It's all been a fearful shock . . . and there's a lot of official work to be dealt with, as you can understand, so if you'd just be good enough to ask Mrs Carrington to give me a ring, when she has a moment, and let me know when it might be convenient to call again?'

'Okay. What's the best time for her to ring you?'

'I'll be home for lunch, if that would suit her; otherwise any time after six o'clock. It's quite urgent. At least, I'm not sure, but I think it might be, otherwise I wouldn't be troubling her in this way. Thanks ever so much.'

'How very mysterious!' I remarked to Robin, as we went

107

indoors. 'What could he possibly have to say to Elsa which is so private and confidential that it can't be said on the telephone? Still, it's one up to him, wouldn't you say?'

'That he has something private and confidential to say to Elsa?'

'No, the fact that we found him standing outside the front door.'

'Honestly, Tessa, I can't see why that should count in his favour.'

'Well, look at it this way. Apart from the Carringtons and the Macadams and the Hearnes and probable various other people who were being ground into the dust by the Trelawney heel, who, apart from them, had the best motive for killing her?'

Since he evidently regarded the question as rhetorical, I supplied the answer myself. 'Who else but this grandson? You could say that he fulfills all the necessary conditions, including opportunity and motive.'

'What motive?'

'Why, Pettits estate and all the money that goes with it. I bet we'll find he was her principal, if not her sole heir, and haven't you always told me that financial gain is invariably the incentive for these planned, premeditated murders?'

'So what difference does his standing outside the front door make to that?'

'It shows that he is not familiar with the customs of the house. Assuming, as we do, that the murderer and the driver of Marc's car are the same person, then that person must have known about the spare set of keys and also that it was usually possible, even when the whole family was away from home, to open the door and walk inside. Presumably, David Trelawney does not know that, otherwise he would not have been standing there just now, with his finger on the bell.'

'Knowing is one thing, putting the knowledge into practice quite another. He might have sneaked in when he knew for certain everyone was out and he was perfectly safe, but he's not on particularly friendly terms with them, I gather, and he may well have thought twice before walking in uninvited, if there was any danger of being caught in the act.'

'In normal circumstances, yes, but he made a great noise about having something urgent and confidential to say to Elsa and surely that must have been true, otherwise he's going to be in quite a jam when she does ring up to ask what it's all about. So when no one answered the doorbell and if he'd found himself without pen and paper to hand, wouldn't the obvious and quite permissable thing have been to have gone inside and written a note for her, if he'd realised the door would be open?'

'Maybe. I find it increasingly difficult to guess what anyone will do in any circumstances, specially when I know so little about them, but then, as it happens, I don't consider you made out a particularly good case against him, in the first place.'

'His motive, you mean? What's wrong with it?'

'Nothing much, if his grandmother had been twenty years younger, or had threatened to cut him out of her will, or was making his life intolerable. Any combination of those three might have provided a plausible motive, but just look at the reality! She's over seventy, so he had every chance of getting the money while he's still young enough to know how to spend it; and in the meantime life for him was far from rough. A young man who can afford to own and run a car like that can't be kept short of money and there is not even the suggestion that he would have been required to make his home with her after he was married. On the contrary, he has only to suggest that a certain house on the estate would do quite nicely for him and his bride and the incumbent tenants are told to get out. Why the hell would he take such an enormous risk, with so much to lose and virtually nothing to gain?'

I had to acknowledge the logic of this argument, which was disappointing for one who had been secretly hoping all along that David would turn out to be the murderer. Not that I had anything against him personally, but it would have been such a very satisfactory conclusion for the Carrington family, killing two birds with one stone, as it were, and opening the way for Pettits Farm to revert to its former style, in the hands of some well brought up, country loving and congenial owners.

'Things are not always what they seem on the surface,' I countered feebly. 'He might have had some fearful grudge against her that we know nothing about.'

'And, if so, I suppose we may rely on you to ferret it out?' Robin asked, but before I could think of an apt reply to this we were joined by Millie, looking quite clean and tidy for once and having obviously been at work with the brush and comb. I hoped it was not a sign that she considered Robin old enough to be interesting.

'Oh, hallo!' I said, 'You've had a visitor, but he's gone away again. Your mother's out and Marc, I take it, is still in bed?'

'Yes, I know we have and Marc's not still in bed. He's not even in his room, so he's probably gone out too.'

'How did you know?'

'About David Trelawney? Because I saw him. What did he want? Not to invite us to the funeral, by any chance?'

'Not as far as I know. If you saw him, why didn't you let him in?'

'I might have, eventually. I heard the car, you see, so I looked out of my window and saw him walk up to the house, and then I heard him ringing and knocking, but I'd just got out of the bath and I didn't want to see him anyway, so I kept my fingers crossed there'd be someone else around to let him in. Then I saw you and Robin coming in and I knew you'd deal with it in your usual efficient style. What did he want?'

'To speak to your mother. He wouldn't say what it was about.'

'Well, I bet she won't want to know, whatever it is. Nasty little creep!'

'You must bear with me, Millie,' Robin said, 'because I'm a comparative stranger in these parts, but what's so creepy about him? He seemed pleasant enough and I thought it was the Grannie who make all the trouble?'

'That's the general view, but in my opinion he's just as bad as she was and only pretending to be secretly on our side. I expect he's beginning to come out in his true colours now, and wants to tell Ma that he intends to construct a main road through our meadow.'

'I should say you were relatively safe there. Does Elsa share these harsh views?'

'Shouldn't think so, she's always being taken in by people. Besides, she's only met him once, so far as I know.'

'When was that?'

'Oh, right at the beginning, when everyone was tumbling over themselves to be friendly. Ma invited him and his Gran to a party, one of those Sunday morning do's which she occasionally goes in for. Mrs Trelawney didn't turn up, or even answer the invitation, but David put in an appearance and was fearfully gushing and polite. Even offered Mrs Hearne a lift home, when he heard she'd have to walk other-wise, but I expect he just seized on that as an excuse to leave early. It was rather funny, really,' Millie added in the amused and contemptuous tone she so often adopted when speaking of her arch enemy, 'because Diane pricked up her ears at that point and said how her mother was rather nervous about driving in fast cars and might need somebody with her, thereby scrounging a lift for herself as well.'

'And that was the one and only time he came here?'

'Right! They never invited us back, so we more or less dropped it and, personally, I prefer it that way.'

'I still can't see why you've got such a down on him.'

'Partly because, unlike my mother, I do listen to gossip, and I happen to know he's not quite such a nice little boy as he pretends to be. There was one thing in particular I heard.'

'What was that?'

'Oh, the Hearnes again, only this time the gloves were off and he'd left his party manners at home. It was Marigold who told me. She's fairly soppy, but not a bad kid and not a liar, like her big sister, so I expect it's true. She told me that when they got the letter from Mrs Trelawney's solicitor saying that the lease of Orchard House was terminated forth·with and they'd have to go, there was a terrific uproar and they were all screaming and tearing their hair and then one afternoon David called on them. He said he hoped it would be all right to take a look round, because he might want to make a few alterations when he moved in and it would be helpful to know what was needed, so that he could get some builders' estimates and so on. As far as the Hearnes were concerned, it was just about the last straw.'

'Yes, very callous and tactless, I agree.'

'Well, wait, because you haven't heard the half of it. It turned out that he hadn't meant to be callous and tactless at all, or so he said anyway, and when it dawned on him how upset they all were he began falling over himself to apolo·gise. He said it had all been a misunderstanding and he'd never had the slightest clue that they weren't leaving voluntarily. He wouldn't dream of turning them out, now he knew the true circumstances, and they were to forget the whole thing.'

'Well, that doesn't sound too bad! Rather creditable, in fact.'

'If you'd just stop interrupting, Tessa, and let me finish?'

'Okay, go on!'

'Well, after that they all sat back and dried their tears and waited for the solicitor's letter to arrive and tell them that there'd been a mistake and they were free to stay at Orchard House for ever and ever. And you want to know what happened?'

'Yes, please!'

'Nothing, absolutely blank, blank nothing. No letter, no word, complete silence!'

'Really? How strange! Still, I suppose no news could have meant good news? Perhaps he just took it for granted, and assumed they would too, that everything had been called off?'

'That's what Diane thought and so did her father. They're a right pair, those two, skipping through life and seeing silver linings all over the place, but Mrs Hearne wasn't so confident. She's like all muddlers, expecting everyone else to be most frightfully efficient; and when the weeks went by and they still didn't hear anything she got frantic and started going round the bend again. Mr Hearne still went on chirping away that there was nothing to worry about, but in the end Diane decided that something had better be done, so she waylaid David in the field one afternoon and asked him what the hell was going on, except of course she made it a bit more refined than that.'

'I can imagine! What was his refined reply?'

'Oh, he hedged and havered a bit, but the upshot was that nothing at all had changed and his grandmother refused even to discuss it. He'd told her about a million times that he didn't want the bloody house and there were several others which would suit him just as well; and he said he was still working on it and hoping to win through in the end, but just for now it was thumbs down. Of course, he put all the blame on Grannie, but Marigold said Diane had the impression he hadn't really tried all that hard and didn't mean to. So that just shows you what a rat he is! Most people take the attitude that he's just a bit dim and soppy, but I'd say he was mad, bad and very likely dangerous to know. I'm doing Byron for A levels.'

'I expect he'd be pleased to hear it. And that was the last any of them heard about it?'

'Far as I know. Mrs Hearne went on wringing her hands and her husband went on with his Micawber act, beaming at everyone and saying they weren't to worry because the Lord would provide. . . .'

Millie broke off and we all remained silent for a few moments, each no doubt struck by the same thought. It was she who put it into words.

'Quite a joke, actually! I mean, there we all were, saying what an irresponsible old fool he was and all the time he was the only one who'd got it right. What I mean is, if it's true that it was Mrs Trelawney and not David who was so set on turning them out, then you could say that the Lord had provided, couldn't you?'

'You could indeed,' Robin agreed, 'and in his own mysterious way, what's more!'

'Now may we be quite clear about this, Mrs Price? You say that you did not notice a car, or vehicle of any kind, in the vicinity of Sowerley Manor, either when you arrived there at approximately four o'clock on Wednesday afternoon, or when you left, which I understand was twenty minutes to half an hour later?'

On the whole, I was relieved to find that he was still harping on the car, since this, combined with the fact that he had so far made no attempt to get in touch with Elsa, revived the hope that the red sports model had now been positively identified as belonging to someone other than Marc and therefore that a new approach was under way.

'That's true,' I replied, 'and I suppose it's bad luck, in a sense. It might have been to my advantage to be able to tell you that there was a plain van outside the gate when I left, with two unwashed, murderous looking types skulking inside it.'

'That would have been a little too much to hope for, wouldn't it? Besides, I'm fairly certain that you have no need to produce evidence to exonerate yourself. In fact, the records show your previous activities in this field to have been largely on the side of the law.'

If Robin had been present at the interview, the last observation might have amused him, but he was not. Possibly in compliance with some unwritten law, he had escorted me to Inspector Bledlow's office, exchanged a few remarks with him concerning some regrettable redevelopments in the centre of Dedley and the pestilential protest marchers, and left us alone.

'The fact remains, though,' the Inspector went on, 'that,

apart from the murderer, you may well have been the last person to see Mrs Trelawney alive and anything at all you can tell us would be of help. So let us go back to this Council visitor she was expecting. Did you, for instance, get any idea whether it was a man or a woman, or whether indeed there was more than one of them?'

'I do remember that both she and the one she called Alice referred to someone from the Council, so I feel fairly sure they meant it in the singular. I can't be certain about the first part of your question. I recall Mrs Trelawney saying she'd make short work of him, but that doesn't necessarily prove she was expecting a man, and, in any case, since neither man nor woman existed and the spurious appointment was only a ruse to ensure that the gate was left unlocked, I can't see how it really matters.'

'I see! You do know a lot, don't you?'

'Mrs Macadam, who also employs Alice, is a great friend of the Carringtons, where I'm staying.'

'Yes, so she is; and you are correct, in a sense. Neverthe-less, spurious or not, somebody must have telephoned to make that appointment and we are naturally anxious to find out everything we can about him or her. I say telephoned, incidentally, because it is most unlikely that there would have been anything in writing.'

'And I'm afraid I'm not being much help to you.'

'Never mind, you have borne out Alice Hawkins' story, which is one bit of clutter out of the way and there are still a few further points I'd like to go over with you. For a start and from the little you knew of her, would you say that Mrs Trelawney's mood was in any way abnormal or apprehen-sive, when she was talking to you?'

'From the little I knew of her and from the great deal more that I've learnt about her since I arrived here, I should say it was one hundred per cent normal and in no way appre-hensive. On the contrary, she was bombastic, aggressive and thoroughly delighted with herself. I don't imagine she was ever afraid of anything or anyone in her life, and that may have been because she hadn't much imagination. Still, that's only an opinion.'

'So no reservations at all regarding this impending visit?'

'Absolutely none. One had the impression that it was the visitor who ought to be feeling nervous. And, anyway, the facts bear that out, don't they? She would hardly have sent Alice away, leaving herself alone in that isolated place, with the gate unlocked, if she believed she had anything to fear?'

The Inspector neither concurred in this, nor disputed it. He remained silent for a moment or two, fiddling with his pen and watching me thoughtfully, before saying, 'Did she mention her grandson at any time?'

'No, she didn't. Do you think he killed her?'

'We are keeping an open mind about that, as well as a good many other questions, at this juncture, but, according to your report, she appears to have confided in you about her family and past rather more freely than was usual with her. I wondered if you had been able to pick up any hints about that particular relationship?'

'I'm afraid it wasn't mentioned, but anyone who knew anything at all about them will tell you that she doted on him. If she had a weakness, it was the boy David. He had but to ask and it was granted.'

'Yes, that does seem to be the general opinion, but from your personal knowledge you can neither confirm nor contradict it?'

'Perhaps in a minor way I can help you confirm it,' I admitted reluctantly, annoyed to find myself manipulated into speaking up on David Trelawney's behalf, which was the last thing I desired. 'There was a photograph. You must have noticed it because it provided the one and only splash of colour in that dreary room. It was a picture of Mrs Trelawney standing between a rather good-looking girl wearing jodhpurs and a fair-haired young man, who I assumed to be her grandson; correctly, as it turns out. They were standing with arms linked and grinning like mad. I know people can put on an act like that when there's a camera pointing at them, but I don't believe she'd have kept it where she did, in a place of honour and the only personal, non-functional object in the room, if it hadn't had great sentimental value for her, do you?'

Far from looking as though he agreed with me and was enjoying our little chat, the Inspector now adopted a most unexpectedly curt, official tone. 'Just a minute, if you please, Mrs Price! Where did you say you saw this photograph?'

'It was all by itself, on a table between the windows.'

'I see,' he said, humming to himself in a tuneless, slightly menacing fashion and at the same time turning over some pages in a yellow folder, which was lying open on the desk in front of him, then finding the one he was searching for and running his finger down the top ten or twelve lines, 'On a table between the windows?'

'That's right. I'm not making it up, you know.'

'Now, why should I suppose anything of the kind?'

'Because something tells me that it was no longer there when your men arrived on the scene?'

'Apparently not, but that's a small point. It will turn up in due course, no doubt. Now, if you'd just be good enough to give me the full description again. . . .'

'He was trying to shrug it off,' I told Robin, as we drove back to Pettits Grange, 'but I could see that he felt it must have some significance and I agree with him. Why else would it have been removed, and by the murderer, presumably? It depresses me to tell you that I have to regard it as yet another point in favour of that tiresome David Trelawney.'

'Why?'

'Because, as I was decent enough to point out in his defence, it was evidence of a kind that he was on rattling good terms with his grandmother, which can hardly fail to do him a bit of good. The fact that he had the best opportunity of anyone wouldn't be enough without some sort of motive or circumstantial evidence to back it up. Isn't that so?'

'Yes, but after all, the murder wasn't set up in a way to

throw suspicion on him or anyone else. It was obviously intended to be seen as an ordinary, routine sort of break-in, where the poor old victim put up a stiffer resistance than the thieves had bargained for, and got clobbered for her pains. So why shouldn't walking off with the photograph, along with the transistor and so on, have been part of that charade?'

'Except that the transistor and so on, unlike the photograph, did have a certain value. It didn't have a silver frame and it wasn't worth a cent. Not even a novice burglar would have been tempted.'

'So what's your explanation?'

'I haven't one. None of it seems to make sense and there are far too many loose ends and unrelated themes. In fact, as far as I can see, only one constructive item has emerged, as yet.'

'Well, better than nothing, I suppose. What is it?'

'I may have found a title for Toby's play. I can't see it pulling them in exactly, but in view of the fact that this is the second photograph to vanish without a trace, I shall suggest that he calls it *Double Negative*.'

SATURDAY P.M.

Millie met us at the door. 'Mind how you go!' she said and started dragging us back down the drive again, 'Ma's in a spin.'

'Why? What's happened? Did the police come?'

'Yes. Not the Inspector, another one. I think he was a sergeant, but he wore ordinary clothes.'

'Was he nasty?'

'Not specially, not at first, anyway. She took Robin's advice and told all. And, incidentally, she's now told me. All those silly lies about Marc's car! She must be mad!'

'How did the sergeant take it?' I asked, wondering whether Inspector Bledlow had deliberately despatched his underling at a time when he had the best of reasons for knowing that Robin and I would be off the premises.

'He was sort of non-commital about it, I gather. I was told to get lost, you may be sure, but Ma said he wrote everything down and then told her he'd make his report and either he or his Inspector might want to see her again at some point.'

'That doesn't sound too bad. So what's the panic?'

'Oh, that was just for starters. The next thing was that he wanted to know whether it would be convenient to talk to Marc.'

'Oh dear! And then what?'

'Ma said she was frightfully sorry, but he was out. He'd left while she was doing the shopping and she'd no idea where he'd gone, or what time he'd be back. She told me she had the definite impression he didn't exactly believe her, but it happened to be true.'

'So then what?'

'The sergeant asked if they could step outside to the garage and see if his car had gone too.'

'And had it?'

'Yes, but that still wasn't the end of it. He then made her go up to Marc's room and try to get some idea of what he'd taken with him and what he'd been wearing when he left. Like, for instance, if his London suit wasn't there, it might indicate that that was where he'd gone. As far as anyone knows, Marc doesn't possess a London suit, he's certainly never been seen in one, but she thought it wouldn't do any good to start arguing about it, so up she trotted.'

'Any results?'

'Well, yes, there were, as a matter of fact, but not the right kind. Like I told you, we're in a bit of a mess. She didn't bother to look through his clothes, or any of that, because the first thing she saw was this note propped up on his dressing table.'

'Oh, crumbs! Saying what?'

'She'll read it to you, but it more or less sent her into hysterics. Anyway, she shoved it in a drawer and went downstairs again and told the sergeant she hadn't a clue what Marc had taken. His room was in its normal state of chaos and, as far as she could tell, he was wearing the clothes he'd changed into when he arrived here yesterday evening. So then he asked her to be sure and let him know the minute Marc returned, which she promised faithfully to do and off he went. That was about ten minutes ago, which is how long it took her to fill me in with the background and she's now gone upstairs to fetch the letter. That's the summary, so far. New readers begin here.'

'See what you make of it,' Elsa said, handing it to Robin.

'It might save time, if you were to read it aloud,' he suggested.

'And you think time is important? Very well, this is what he says: *Dear Ma, Have decided to go away on my own for a few days, to cool off and try and work out what I'm going to do about D. Sorry to break the news so dramatically, but everyone seems to be either out or asleep, and I don't feel like hanging about. I'll be in touch and, for God's sake, don't worry. Love, Marc.*

'Don't worry, he says,' she remarked bitterly, folding the letter and putting it in her pocket. 'That wretched girl! I could strangle her. How could she do this to him and at such a moment?'

'To be fair, she wasn't to know that it would be the moment for him to become entangled with the police.'

'I wasn't thinking of that so much. It seemed to me that she could at least have waited until his exams were over, but you're right, of course. Just now, there are worse things to worry about. What should I do, Robin?'

'Let's start, shall we, by removing some of the under-growth? I don't know whether you agree, but it sounds to me as though he hasn't begun to realise that he is in any tangle. Otherwise he surely wouldn't have been such a damn fool as to have gone hopping off, without leaving an address?'

'I agree with you absolutely. He hasn't a single idea in his head except this tiresome girl. I blame her entirely.'

'So it follows,' Robin went on, 'that he regards the car episode as some temporary misunderstanding and assumes also that you have now supplied the necessary proof concerning the flat battery and that all is not only well, but is seen to be well?'

'Of course, he does, and so it would be, if it weren't for those stupid lies I told. It's entirely my own idiotic, unforgivable lack of trust which has landed him in this absurd situation.'

'That's not quite true, so don't waste time blaming yourself. You may have compounded the evil, but the fact would still remain that someone must have seen and recognised his car that afternoon. He would still have had to fight his way out of that one.'

'But at least it would have been straightforward. He would have understood what he was up against and he wouldn't have gone dashing off into the blue like this. The horribly ironic thing is that, whereas all of us take that as positive proof of his innocence, the people in charge of the case are bound to see it as an indication of guilt, aren't they?'

'Yes, I'm afraid they may, but we still have a little time left to us before that happens, an hour or two, anyway. I suggest we use them in the most practical way we can.'

'And what would that be?'

'Well, I'm a bit of a washout here, but why don't you and Millie concentrate on all the places where he might be and, if you have any luck there, the next job will be to try and persuade him to come home with the least possible delay. It's now just after one, so he's had four or five hours' start.'

'Well, obviously, not London,' Elsa said, 'although I suppose we can't afford to ignore any possibility, however remote.'

'And anyway why "obviously"?' Robin asked.

'Because at the moment London is associated with work and all the hard grind of study, which is the last sort of atmosphere he'd be looking for, if he wanted to resolve some emotional problem. A second objection, paradoxically enough, is that he'd expect me to try there first, which is all too clearly another reason to rule it out.'

While her mother was speaking, Millie had picked up the telephone and dialled nine digits. In the silence which followed she shook her head and a moment or two later replaced the receiver, without comment.

'Right!' Robin said. 'We appear to have crossed London off the list. What's next?'

'How about Bexhill?' I suggested.

'Oh no, do you really think so, Tessa? I mean, in a small bungalow, and with her mother and aunt there too? It would be cramped, to say the least.'

'You were the one to say we couldn't afford to leave out any possibility.'

'Yes, I know, but . . . oh, very well, but I don't know the number, or even the aunt's name. You'd better ring up Orchard House, Millie, and find out.'

'What excuse shall I make?'

'Oh goodness, I don't know. Surely you can think of something?'

'If you can't, how the hell am I supposed to be able to?'

'Now, Millie, don't get rattled, please!' Robin warned her. 'Cool heads and long tempers are what we require now.'

Rather to my relief, she accepted the rebuke without protest and I said, 'You dial and I'll do the talking, if you like?'

Luckily, it was Marigold who answered and I put on a funny voice and asked whether it would be convenient to speak to Miss Diane Hearne.

'I'm sorry, she's not here at present.'

'Could you tell me where I can get in touch with her? It's rather urgent.'

'Well, no, I'm afraid it's a bit difficult ... who is it speaking?'

'This is Pettits Farm estate office. I have a message for Miss Hearne from Mr David Trelawney. It's important.'

'What? I don't understand ... are you sure? Did you say David Trelawney?'

'That's right.'

'But there must be some mistake ... surely. . . .'

'No, no mistake, and if you'd just tell me where I can get in touch with Miss Hearne?'

'No, I can't. She'll be on the train by now.'

'On the train?'

'To Victoria. Do you want her to ring you when she gets here?'

'No, the office will be closed this afternoon. I'll have to leave it till Monday. She will be there on Monday, I take it?'

'Oh yes, but. . . .'

'Thanks so much. Goodbye.'

'Poor Marigold,' I said, putting the receiver back, 'she was knocked all of a heap.'

'And no wonder!'

'I'm afraid there'll be worse to come, if they try to find out what it's all about on Monday. Still, what matters, from our point of view, is that we've drawn another blank. Diane is on her way to Victoria, so if Marc ever went to Bexhill, he's certainly left again by now. Next, please!'

'What an extraordinary thing to do, though!' Elsa said. 'Whatever gave you the idea of using David Trelawney's name?'

'I rather regret it now. The poor creature sounded absolutely aghast and appalled. I suppose she thought the message was to say they'd got to get out of the house next week. Though why the hell she should have I don't know. In the circumstances, it could equally well have been a reprieve. Anyway, it had to be somebody they couldn't call back, not immediately at any rate, and I suppose it was the young man himself who gave me the idea that he would do as well as anyone.'

'David Trelawney?'

'Yes. If he has something urgent to communicate to you, why shouldn't he have something equally urgent to say to Diane?'

'Would you mind telling me what you're talking about, Tessa?'

'He called here this morning, asking to see you on a matter of urgency. Didn't Millie tell you?'

'No.'

'Didn't get a chance, did I? What with the fuzz bursting in on us. . . .'

'What did he want?'

'He wasn't telling. Only that he'd like you to ring him up and make an appointment, either before lunch or at about six this evening. You're too late for the first and much too early for the second, so there's nothing to be done about it, for the time being.'

'It's so puzzling, though. What on earth can he have to say to me which involves so much secrecy? We've scarcely exchanged more than a dozen words since he came here.'

'Well, all will be revealed in due course, I daresay, and, in the meantime, shouldn't we be pressing on with our own very urgent business? Try and think of some of the other places where Marc might be.'

Almost the whole of the next two hours was spent in

putting through telephone calls to points throughout the United Kingdom, most of them being conducted, in various guises, by myself, Elsa claiming that she would feel such a fool having to ask all these friends and relatives if they knew where her son was, and at the end of it we were not one inch further forward.

'Well, that's it, as far as I can see,' she said. 'We've scraped the bottom of the barrel now and it's obvious that he meant exactly what he said. He wanted to go away somewhere on his own, while he sorts things out, and he's taken good care to choose a place where we should never dream of looking for him. Our only hope is that he'll have come to some decision and be back at work again on Monday.'

Robin did not comment, but I guessed from his expression that he doubted whether Monday would be quite soon enough to suit Inspector Bledlow. If so, he was absolutely right, because the next time I intercepted a call it had come from that very gentleman. He was ringing to enquire whether there had been any word from Marc, only this time, according to Elsa, in distinctly more grave and threatening terms than hitherto. This was not altogether surprising, in view of the fact that the red sports car had now been located, with no entry ticket on display, in the Municipal car park behind Dedley railway station.

'The maddening part of it is,' I remarked to Robin, on our way to the golf course later that afternoon, 'every single move that boy makes, however much it may confirm his innocence to us, only adds one more nail to the coffin which Inspector Bledlow is building for him. If there is one sure way to draw attention to yourself in this world it is to get a summons for illegal parking. What can have possessed him to do such a thing?'

'In a hurry to catch his train, no doubt.'

'Yes, and that's not going to look very good, is it? What construction are they going to put on that?'

'Presumably, the car having now become a well known,'

not to say notorious, feature in the case, that he was anxious to put as much distance as possible between it and himself.'

'Precisely! Although even they must realise that his chances of increasing the distance would have been a lot bigger if he had paid the parking fee.'

'They will assume that he panicked.'

'So what now? Will there be a warrant out for his arrest? Bloodhounds at all the airports and channel ferries and so on?'

'I expect so.'

'And they're bound to catch up with him eventually, aren't they? How long would you give it?'

'Well, as you've just pointed out, he's not being terribly bright, is he? Judging on current form, I'd say twenty-four hours, at the most.'

'It's a pretty formidable task,' I remarked sadly.

'What is?'

'Two, really. The first one, naturally, to find out where he is and get him back, before the police do it for us.'

'And the second?'

'That may be even tougher, seeing how short is the time at our disposal. It is to find and obtain proof of just who did murder Mrs Trelawney.'

In the days that followed I was able to make my contribution towards furthering both these ends, but, even before the first step along the way had been taken, news had reached us which for the time being pushed even Marc's danger into the background. Before nine o'clock on Sunday morning we learned that, in the view of at least one person, Mrs Trelawney had claimed her second victim, or third if you counted Daisy, the retriever; only this time from beyond the grave.

SUNDAY A.M.

The murder of Mrs Trelawney had received scant attention in the national press, vicious attacks on elderly women living in solitary state being unhappily all too common, and had been greeted by most of her neighbours with indifference or varying degrees of silent relief.

It was not so with the death, by her own hand, of sixteen-year-old Marigold Hearne, although it was not until Monday morning that the full impact of the Fleet Street invasion began to impinge on the village.

One of the worst aspects of that shattering event was the manner of its discovery. Soon after dawn on Sunday morning Mrs Hearne, much improved in health and spirits after her three days at the seaside, and mooching about in the long, dewy grass, as was her habit on those days when she felt optimistic enough to haul herself out of bed at all, had perceived what she took to be a sackful of something or other, suspended from the branch of an apple tree.

Realising as time went by, that this was a strange place for it to be and, furthermore, that someone had been thoughtless enough to leave an upturned kitchen stool directly underneath it, she had moved closer until eventually, with some of the last remnants of sanity which she was to retain for several months, recognised it for what it was.

She had, in fact, remained just coherent enough to give some sort of wild account of the affair to her husband and elder daughter, but shortly afterwards had collapsed completely and, by the time the news reached Pettits Grange, had been moved back into the psychiactric ward.

'Not wishing to be callous in any way, but perhaps it will at least give us a little breathing space,' I suggested to Robin, striving to wrest one ray of cheerfulness from this dismal tale. 'I daresay Inspector Bledlow does not often have to cope

127

with two violent deaths in the space of a few days, so presumably the resources and personnel are somewhat stretched at the moment?'

'And if this one should turn out to be murder and not suicide, they would be stretched still further and you would be more pleased than ever?'

'Well, I wouldn't go so far as to say that and, in any case, a delay of ten or twelve hours is all I'm asking for.'

'You think Marc will have come back of his own accord by then?'

'I'm not banking on it, but I've found one more card in my hand and it just might turn out to be the ace.'

'Really? How did it get there?'

'I'd been puzzling about the style of his departure and I couldn't make out why he should have gone by train, when he had a perfectly good car to travel in. When we discussed it yesterday we agreed that the police would see it as a desire to dump the car as soon as possible, because without it he would be so much less conspicuous, but you and I know that this cannot be the true explanation. He doesn't have the least idea that he is wanted for questioning in connection with the murder and therefore it would never have occurred to him that the car could be any sort of hindrance or embarrassment. So the question remains: why go by train?'

'And you believe you have found the answer?'

'I've thought of one answer and, if it's right, it will at least tell us where he is. The trouble is that I can't put it to the test until I've checked out a few points with Millie.'

'So what's stopping you?'

'There hasn't been a chance yet. Elsa has snatched her up to go and collect the three youngest Hearne children. She thinks it will be more wholesome for them to spend the day here than being stuck in all that misery at home, and she also thinks she is more likely to get a favourable response to the proposal if she's accompanied by a member of the younger generation. Personally, I regard it as a great mistake. I mean I quite realise that she's a compulsive do-gooder and couldn't

128

stop rushing about and handing out crutches to lame dogs, if she tried, but I think the mistake is in dragging Millie in and trying to make her a part of it. In fact, in my opinion, this close-knit little family unit she strives so hard to weld them all into is defeating its own object. I'm sure the children find it stifling at times and you notice what comes of it? The minute Marc's love life starts falling about him in ruins, his one ambition is to put as much distance between himself and his mother as he possibly can and to make damn sure she doesn't find out where he is.'

'Ah well, it's never hard to see where other people go wrong in bringing up their children. When you have a family of your own, you may find all these clear cut values and opinions becoming a little frayed round the edges.'

Luckily, I was spared the necessity of having to answer the unanswerable, because at that moment Elsa and Millie walked in, *sans* Hearne children. The mission, it seemed, had not been an unqualified success, although, according to Elsa, by no means a total failure either.

'At least, poor James had an opportunity to talk and bring it out into the open, which I felt must have done him some good. And Millie was such a brick! She took the children out to the garden and read them a story, so that he and I could be alone for a while. I really do feel that, at a time like this, lending a sympathetic ear is probably the best way to help someone.'

'And where was Diane while all this was going on?'

'At the hospital. They won't allow her to see her mother, she's under sedation, but Diane feels she ought to be there, in case she's needed, so I gather she means to spend the whole day more or less camping out in the waiting room.'

'Wouldn't you know?' Millie asked.

'Well, perhaps people react in different ways when they are faced with a catastrophe of this magnitude,' Elsa said, sounding only mildly reproachful. 'James was talking rather a lot of twaddle too, but I didn't take it seriously.'

'What kind of twaddle?'

'Oh, things like how it was God's will that Marigold should be taken from us; that we should all be so thankful because, however much some people might say that she had sinned in taking her own life, she had died in purity and innocence and would never have to experience all the sorrows and tribulations of a suffering world. Rather nauseating, really, but poor man! I daresay it consoles him to believe such rubbish.'

'So he has no doubt at all that it was suicide?' Robin asked, with a glance at me.

'Oh, none whatever. After all, what else could it be?'

'And did he have any ideas about why she might have done it?'

'We didn't go very deeply into that, but I gather he attributes it entirely to this wretched business of having to move out of Orchard House and all the uncertainty of where they will go. I suppose one must accept that he is right. It would scarcely be credible as a rational motive in a normal sixteen-year-old, but presumably Marigold had inherited rather more of her mother's instability than appeared on the surface.'

'That's not the view that Matthew and Bernadette take,' Millie said. 'I don't know about Rosie, she's probably too dim and retarded to take it in, but I wasn't reading stories all the time, because the other two were also quite keen to talk about Marigold.'

'You mean they've been told how she died?'

'They were there when Mrs Hearne came screeching into the house, saying that she'd hanged herself. Diane tried to palm them off with another version later on, told them that Marigold had fallen out of a tree, or something, but they aren't that stupid.'

'So why do they think it wasn't losing the house that made her do it?' I asked. 'What's their theory?'

'Well, they admit she'd been worried sick about something for the past week or two. In fact, she'd been having screaming nightmares and one morning Bernadette found her lying on her bed, howling; only when she asked her what was the matter, Marigold said she couldn't tell anyone, it was a secret and anyway they wouldn't understand and all she wanted was to be left alone.'

'Well, there you are, then!' Elsa said.

'No I'm not, because, like they said, if it was the house she was worrying about, that was no secret and also she'd got it back to front. That saga has been going on for months now and she'd never appeared to be any more upset than the rest of them, so why should it hit her like this now? With Mrs Trelawney dead, there's a fair chance that they won't have to move out, after all, so this is the time for cheering up a bit, not for hanging yourself.'

'And they certainly have a point there,' I agreed. 'So what's their theory?'

'They haven't got one, or if they have they're keeping it to themselves. All they know is that Marigold has been getting more and more depressed for about a week now and yesterday afternoon she was in a complete state of jitters. It ended with her refusing to come downstairs for supper, even though it was her mother's and Diane's first evening back at home. So would you care to hear what construction I put on it?'

Elsa looked as though it were quite the last thing she would care to hear and was about to say as much, in paraphrased form, so I jumped in quickly.

'Yes, Millie, I certainly would.'

'I'd say it was all on account of that batty mother. Marigold just couldn't stand the misery and insecurity of never knowing what kind of mood she was going to be in and what kind of mess it would have landed them in by the end of the day. I expect her coming back yesterday, after three lovely days of freedom, was the last straw and Marigold decided she just couldn't take any more.'

I was interested by this assessment which, to my mind, although inadequate as an explanation for suicide, was probably somewhat nearer the mark than the one put forward by James Hearne, and found myself silently eating

131

my own words rather sooner than might have been forseen. On this occasion, Elsa had unquestionably done the wise thing in involving Millie in her charitable activities. However, I could not spare the time to reflect further on this, any more than on the glimmer of an idea which had now flashed into my mind concerning the murder, because Millie's disclosures had evidently provided Elsa and Robin with food for thought too, bringing a lull into the conversation and providing me with the chance I had been waiting for.

'Remind me of something, Millie,' I said. 'You remember when you were telling your mother and me about Geoffrey taking you to stay with his sister in Somerset?'

'Yes?'

'You said that you went by train and that he and Marc put up at an hotel called the George & Dragon? Right?'

'Right!'

'You wouldn't happen to remember where it was, the name of the village or town, by any chance?'

'Wouldn't I, though! It was two or three miles from where Gertrude lived, at a place called Pissminster. Marc and I were of an age to find that frightfully funny. Geoffrey was faintly shocked by our giggles and went into long explanations about how it had something to do with the history of the Church, which made us laugh all the more. That's how I remember it.'

'And do you think Marc would remember it just as clearly?'

'Oh, sure! One way and another, it made quite an impression.'

'Have you got an AA book, Elsa?'

'Yes, in the drawer of my desk, I think. Do you want me to look up the George & Dragon at Pissminster?'

'It might be worth a try.'

'So that's where you think Marc might have got to?' Robin asked.

'It has all the right ingredients, hasn't it? A place he knows

132

and remembers with affection, and yet at the same time where it wouldn't occur to anyone to look for him. There can't be many such, can there? Incidentally, Millie, which station did you travel to when you went there with Geoffrey?'

'Bath. Gertrude met us there in her car and drove us around all the pump rooms and things for about two hours. She and Geoffrey kept quoting bits from Jane Austen, so that's imprinted on my memory too.'

'And you're doing very well! Better and better, in fact, because Bath is on the same line as Dedley, which suggests to me that Marc didn't ditch the car through fear of making himself an easy target, but because this was also to be something in the nature of a sentimental journey and every step along the way had to be an exact copy of the first time, even to going by rail and perhaps having a nostalgic look at Bath on the way. I honestly do think it's worth a try.'

'I agree with you,' Elsa said, getting up and leaving the room.

She was away for a full ten minutes, during which Robin leant sideways, so as to be able to read the Sunday paper without actually picking it up, while Millie yawned at least five times and made a few more inroads on the box of choco-lates which he had most ill-advisedly brought her from London.

'Did you ever discover what David Trelawney wanted to see her about?' I asked.

'No, she said she had enough trouble on her hands, as it was, without taking on his as well, and if it was so damned urgent he could damn well lift the telephone himself. Rather strong words, for her, weren't they? Anyway, I imagine she forgot the whole thing when she heard about Marigold.'

'I expect so,' I agreed, 'and, presumably, it can't have been so very urgent, after all, since lifting the telephone is what he hasn't bothered to do.'

'You were quite right, Tessa,' Elsa said, rejoining us at last, 'Your intuition or experience, or both, have paid off once again.'

133

'Hooray! Did you speak to him?'

'No, he was out, but he hasn't left yet. He told the desk that he'll be staying until tomorrow morning. I asked them to give him a message. I said they were to tell him not to worry, but there'd been some very bad news and it was essential that he should call me back the minute he comes in.'

'Will he understand why he doesn't need to worry when the news is so bad?'

'It was the best I could think of. I had to pitch it fairly strong, because the last thing I want is to lose touch with him again, now that we have caught up, but at the same time I was trying to convey that nothing terrible had happened to Millie or me.'

'Perhaps we should let Bledlow know,' Robin said, dragging his eyes from the newspaper. 'I imagine he'll be spending this pleasant Sunday morning in his hot little office.'

'I've already done that, Robin. That's partly what took me so long. I told him. . . .' Elsa broke off, looking sheepish and uncomfortable.

'What?'

'I thought it would sound better if I said that Marc had got in touch with me of his own accord. There couldn't be any harm in that, could there? Anyway, that's what I did and I also said that he would be back here this evening.'

'You're confident he'll come then?'

'Yes, because I'm not going to mention anything at all about the police until he gets here. When he does call me back I shall simply tell him about Marigold and that'll do it. He'll come tearing back by the first train, in case Diane needs him, you see if he doesn't!'

'Clever thinking!' I told her. 'And at least the first of your problems is on the way to being solved. Why aren't you looking happier about it?'

'What? Oh yes, naturally, I'm happy about it, very happy indeed. It's just that something else has cropped up and it worries me a little.'

'What now?'

'Well, you see, I keep the AA manual in what we call the car drawer of my desk, along with the insurance certificates and so on, and also that spare set of keys.'

'Which are no longer there?'

'Oh, but they are, you see! Back in their right place, where they belong. It's completely illogical, of course, but for some reason that worries me almost more than their being taken away. There's something going on which I don't understand and I don't care for it at all.'

SUNDAY P.M.

'At least, you can't complain that there's not enough plot,' I remarked to Toby, as we relaxed in his summer house before dinner on Sunday evening. Robin had been obliged to return to London soon after tea and had been unable to avail himself of the invitation, which had included the whole party and had reached us just after Elsa's revelation concerning the car keys. She too had naturally asked to be excused, as she did not intend to budge from the house until Marc was safely back in the fold; but, since I was beginning to find the atmosphere at the Grange somewhat oppressive and since also the dinner was to be in celebration of Mrs Parkes' return, I asked if there would be any objection to my going on my own. In fact, she had been all in favour of it, relieved at this stage, I imagine, not to have to struggle with dishing up another meal, and, as an afterthought, had asked if it would be an awful bore to take Millie as well.

'It will make things so much easier if she's not here when Marc does get back,' she explained. 'Otherwise, sooner or later, she'll start teasing and picking on him and everything will get completely out of hand.'

Naturally, I had agreed to this, although reminding her that the Parkes menu was unlikely to conform very closely to Millie's notions of the civilised person's diet, to which she replied, rather heartlessly for her, that this was of no consequence.

'She's been gorging herself on chocolates the whole weekend, so a little forcible fasting is probably what she needs.'

As it turned out, however, Millie was not to suffer this terrible fate, and when she learnt that some of Toby's special late strawberries were to figure on the menu she gallantly offered to pick them herself and to help Mrs Parkes with the hulling, thus providing me with the opportunity to bring Toby up to date with recent developments.

'It's not the absence of plot which bothers me,' I went on. 'On the contrary, there seems to be almost too much of it. The real trouble is that none of it hangs together.'

'I tend to agree with you. In fact, I begin to sense my audience losing the thread and becoming a little restive at this point.'

'Well, I hope there are enough threads for some of them to cling on to at least one; and, if I were writing it, I should now start to put the emphasis on the missing photographs.'

'And what is so significant about them?'

'The fact that they stick out like two identical sore thumbs, one on each hand, and are therefore likely to be attached to the same pair of arms. That's one thing that seems to set them apart. Another is that, however senseless and baffling the removal of those photographs may appear to us, to someone else it must have made very good sense indeed. Whereas everything else that's happened either was or could have been inadvertent and, given the slapdash attitude to premises and property which exists in the Carrington household, could still be found to have an innocent explanation. In this category I include the temporary disappearance of the keys and the fact that someone borrowed the car. Not so the photographs; they must have been taken for a specific purpose. That's why I feel so strongly that if we could only find out who did take them and why, we should have all the answers.'

'Ah well, perhaps it's a little early for that. We're only just into Act Two, you know, and the dénouement is still some way off. In the meantime, how were all the other threads tangling themselves up when you left this evening?'

'Marc telephoned just after lunch. Of course, the first thing he wanted to know was how Elsa had managed to dig him out, but she side-tracked that and went straight into the sad tale of Marigold. That rocked him completely, as she had known it would and he told her he'd get the five o'clock train, which stops at Dedley. She was going over to meet him because, of course, his car won't be there. Actually, as I need hardly say, it's been impounded by the police, who are going over it, inch by inch, with powerful microscopes, but she didn't mention that. She simply said it had been towed away because of illegal parking.'

'All of which rather suggests to me that she wouldn't trust him to come back, if he knew the police were beating on his door, but, as you say, we probably have enough threads in our hands already, without adding to them. What about the suicide?'

'Not a lot. Robin spoke to Inspector Bledlow before he left, but he didn't get much out of him. Only that there appears to be not one shred of evidence to indicate that it was anything other than suicide.'

'Oh, that's a blow!'

'Yes, but I'm afraid we're stuck with it. She even left a note.'

'Did she indeed? And what did that say?'

'Robin couldn't tell me the exact wording, but it was plain enough to leave no doubts. It was in a sealed envelope, addressed to Diane, and it seems that one of the younger children found it.'

'Where?'

'In a broken down outhouse which they use as a sort of games room. That was a strange place to leave it, wasn't it? Perhaps it does indicate that she was really quite unbalanced. Or do you suppose she put it there in the hope of ensuring that it was read by Diane alone? Not by her father, for instance?'

'Was there anything about him in it?'

'Not as far as I know. It was simply to the effect that she couldn't stand living under the terrible strain any longer and she knew Diane would understand and forgive her. Terribly pathetic, really. Millie thinks this strain she was living under was caused by her mother's dottiness, but I have another idea about that. In any case, if her last wish was that only

Diane should read it, she was thwarted in that too, because it appears that Diane immediately telephoned the Inspector, who immediately sent one of his minions to collect it. So it will doubtless be read aloud at the inquest and probably figure on the front page of *The Dedley Mercury* as well.'

'Still, I hardly see that she could have suppressed it.'

'Don't you? There are such things as garden incinerators, you know, not to mention pottery kilns. Perhaps I've been infected by Millie's prejudice, but it sounds to me as though Diane didn't give a damn about respecting her sister's last wishes, and all she minded about was getting it clearly estab-lished as suicide. The fact that it was marked Private and Confidential didn't bother her for one minute.'

'But you don't suggest that it was a forgery?'

'No, I don't. It's just that I got the impression, talking to her, that fundamentally Marigold was probably as sane as most people and therefore she may have had a much more rational motive for killing herself than she chose to reveal. And what depresses me most is that I doubt if we shall ever find out . . . oh, hallo!' I said, switching to the jolly prefect voice, as Millie came plunging into the summer house and collapsed on to a cane chaise longue. 'You look hot and a trifle bothered.'

As it happened, she looked several other things as well, including heavily stained round the mouth and chin, but I had been careful to choose two of the least offensive epithets which came to mind.

'I am,' she replied gloomily, 'and I do think it was perfectly rotten of Robin to bring me those chocolates.'

'I know,' I admitted, 'but it was partly my fault. I forgot to warn him that you were on a diet and I'm afraid he's still apt to think of you as about eight years old. I did suggest that he should take them back and exchange them for something else, but unfortunately there were only about four left by then.'

'And now there are none left and I feel like a Strasbourg goose.'

139

'No, no, that's nonsense! You're not in the least like a Strasbourg goose. You look lovely; most of the time.'

'Well, kindly shut up, because I know I don't and, further-more, I'm very badly adjusted, psychologically.'

'Oh no, you're not . . .' I began but Toby interrupted:

'For God's sake, Tessa, do stop being so bossy and patronising. You're the one who's treating her as though she were eight years old. If she chooses to see herself as a psycho-logically maladjusted goose, that's her business, so don't interfere.'

Toby was now visibly preening himself on the grateful and admiring looks he was getting from Millie for his wisdom and tolerance, and I reminded myself to tell him later that she only valued his opinions because he already had one foot in the grave.

Aloud, I said, 'Okay, I apologise. Just tell us why you think you are and I promise to give you my silent and steadfast attention.'

'Because I can't get it right, whichever way I play it. Some-times I get so choked up by Ma's passion for helping people and mixing herself up in their lives and quite often I have the sneaking feeling that they'd much sooner be allowed to work things out for themselves, which is how I feel when she tries to take my life over. So that makes me go to the opposite extreme and then something like this happens and I feel awful about it.'

'Something like what happens?' Toby asked.

'It's Marigold, really,' she replied, starting to unwind a loose strip of binding on the arm of her chair, which he heroically refrained from protesting about, although I could see it was driving him to the edge of madness.

'What about Marigold?'

'It's what I'm awfully afraid I may have done to her yester-day. It's not only the chocolates and a few strawberries which are making me feel sick. Ever since I heard about Marigold hanging herself I feel sick practically the whole time.'

'There's nothing maladjusted about that,' I assured her,

breaking my vow, 'I imagine we all do.'

'Yes, but at least you lot haven't got all this remorse looming over you. There was nothing you could have done about it.'

'And what makes you believe you could have done anything about it?'

'I don't know whether I could or not. The point is that I didn't bother to find out. I passed by on the other side, you might say.'

'When was this, Millie?'

'Yesterday evening, about five o'clock, I should think. You remember how we'd spent practically the whole afternoon ringing up everyone under the sun who might know where Marc was? In the end I got so fed up with it I could have screamed. It was one of those times when I longed to say, 'He's twenty-two, for God's sake, and not exactly mentally handicapped. Why can't he be left to work out his own problems and ask for your help when he needs it?' Anyway, when we'd run out of people to ring up, Ma went upstairs to rest and you and Robin skipped off somewhere, to the golf course or something, and I decided to work off some of the bad temper by going to see my friend Janie. She's a student at Dedley Art School now, but her parents live in Sowerley and she spends weekends with them. She's very cool and she doesn't ask any questions, unless you're in the mood for them, which I certainly was not. Anyway, the first person I saw when I went out of the gate was Marigold and it was funny, really. I'd never noticed it before, but she looked exactly like her mother. You never met Mrs Hearne, did you, but she has this peculiar way of walking, as though she knew it was important to get where she was going to, only she couldn't remember where it was.'

'And where was Marigold going?'

'Well, that's it, isn't it? That's the awful part about it, because, you see, she can really only have been going to our house, can't she? I mean, after that there isn't anything else except woods and she had plenty of those at home.'

'So what happened?'

'When she saw me she looked sort of scared, at first, then she started to look pleased and she dashed up and said, "Oh, Millie, I'm so glad to see you, I've been so worried . . ." Well, you know, I used to quite like Marigold, she was easily the best of that bunch, but I certainly wasn't feeling in the mood for her just then. Besides, I wanted to get down and see Janie and hear a bit of sense, for a change. So I said, "Sorry, Marigold, can't stop now, I'm in an awful rush", and I walked straight on. So now can you see why I feel such a skunk?'

'Did you look back after you'd left her?'

'Yes, once I did because, you know, I could feel her watch-ing me; like they say in books, her eyes boring into my back. So I turned round and there she was, just standing in the middle of the lane and staring at me. After that I didn't look round again. End of sad story.'

It would have ended there anyway, because Mrs Parkes presented herself in our midst, looking irritatingly sun-tanned and with her hair bleached about four shades lighter than normal. Toby had prepared me for this. 'All carefully created with make-up and hair dye, mark you,' he had told me, 'but it amuses her to rub salt in the wound by pretending that she has been basking in the sun for ten days.'

'Are you ready for us, Mrs Parkes?' he now asked in subservient tones.

'Came to tell you that the soufflé will be on the table in exactly ten minutes. Just time for a nice wash and brush up,' she added, giving Millie a rather straight look, followed by an oblique one at the long strip of cane which now hung in dejected coils from the arm of the chaise longue.

'That's not bad, wouldn't you say?' Toby asked me, as we sauntered back to the house.

'Being in soufflé-land again, you mean?'

'Oh, that too, of course, but I was really referring to the sad little encounter between Millie and Marigold.'

'I didn't notice anything particularly good about it.'

'Not from their point of view, perhaps, and, in fact, it's not quite right as it stands, but I do think it might be worked up into quite a good curtain line for Act Two, Scene One, don't you?'

MONDAY

'Did you ever discover what David Trelawney was so anxious to see you about?' I asked the next morning.

Marc and Millie were still in bed, Marc having been safely tucked up in his since about an hour before our return from dining with Toby on Sunday evening, when it had been quite a relief to learn that he was spending the night in his own room and not a police cell.

Inspector Bledlow had apparently accepted the explanation for his sudden departure as being due to purely personal reasons, having doubtless turned up the fact, in some intervening investigations, that Marc had recently been jilted by his young lady; and doubtless also his so-called voluntary return had counted as another point in his favour. He had been requested not to leave Pettits Grange again, without notifying the police, but otherwise was still a free man.

'Yes, I did,' Elsa replied. 'He rang up just after you and Millie left and asked if he could have my advice about a matter which was bothering him. I wanted to know why he couldn't say whatever it was on the telephone, but he said he didn't think it would be suitable. He sounded a bit pained, as a matter of fact.'

'I expect it was really me he was pained with. Probably thought I'd forgotten to pass on the message.'

'Well, we didn't go into that, but I'd become quite curious to know what all the secrecy was about, by then, so I told him that I had to go into Dedley to meet someone off a train, but that I'd leave ten minutes early and call in on my way.'

'Which you did?'

'Which I did. It was quite one of the most absurd and yet worrying little problems I've ever been required to deal with,' she replied, then drifted off into a kind of dream, so

144

that for a minute or two I was quite afraid that I was now to regard the subject as closed.

However, she then appeared to wake up and, focussing on me again, she said, 'But perhaps I've missed something terribly obvious. You must see what you can make of it.'

'I'll try my best.'

'It's a story about a handkerchief.'

'Oh, really?' I asked, somewhat taken aback by this unexpected opening. 'How quaint!'

'You remember Tim Macadam, Louise's husband?' she then asked, with what appeared to be irrelevance running riot.

'Yes, vividly.'

'Do you know why he's called Tim?'

'I suppose I just sort of took it for granted that it was short for Timothy,' I said, doing my best to keep in step.

Elsa shook her head: 'No, he is called Tim because his irresponsible parents saw fit to have him christened Theodore Ignatius and ever since he was a schoolboy he's been known to his friends as Tim.'

'I quite understand.'

'Good! And perhaps you also remember hearing about Alice Hawkins, who works at Pettits Farm and also for Louise?'

'Yes, Elsa, I do.'

'One of the jobs she does for the Trelawneys, although not for Louise, is the washing and ironing. That is to say, she doesn't take on big things, like sheets and so on, which are sent to the Storhampton laundry, but she does all the small household linen and also personal stuff, such as David's shirts. She's not supposed to do handkerchiefs either, they also go to the laundry, but just occasionally one gets left in a pyjama pocket, or something like that, and finds its way into the machine. So then naturally she irons it and puts it back in his room with the other clean things. Which is more or less what happened last Friday.'

'More or less?'

145

'Unfortunately, there's a slight mystery surrounding this one. Alice doesn't go to Pettits on Thursday, that's her day for Louise, but she was there as usual last Friday. In fact, David told me he'd been down to see her on Thursday evening and had particularly asked her to go, which she consented to, after he'd explained that the police had finished their on-the-spot investigations and everything was back to normal again. In a manner of speaking,' Elsa added, and then fell silent again.

'So she went on Friday,' I prompted, 'and did the washing and ironing?'

'Yes, she collected everything up from the linen baskets in both bathrooms and also from a bin in the kitchen and when David came in that evening he found the clean pile lying on his bed. On top of it was a man's white handkerchief, made of very fine lawn. He knew it wasn't one of his and when he examined it he saw that on one corner there was a tiny embroidered monogram. The initials were M.I.T., or whichever order you care to put them in. He wanted me to advise him what to do about it.'

'Why you?'

'Because his first thought was that he ought to tell the police, but then he saw the significance of those three initials and, since I'm known to be an old and close friend of the Macadams, he decided to consult me first. I can't say I'm grateful to him. It's one of the most odious things I've ever been consulted about in my entire life.'

'Because you also think that's what he should do?'

'I don't know what I think. I suppose if I'm honest with myself, I know that, if it weren't for those blasted initials, I shouldn't hesitate. As it is, I keep beating my brains out to find some good reason why Tim could have left a handkerchief in that house some time between Wednesday morning, when Alice did the mid-week wash, and approximately eight hours later, when the police were called in.'

'Then I should stop beating your brains out this very minute,' I told her, 'because, obviously, what actually happened is that Alice found the handkerchief lying around in the Macadams' house when she was working there on Thursday, absent-mindedly stuffed it in the pocket of her apron or overall, and it was still there when the apron or overall went into the Trelawney washing machine on Friday. What's wrong with that?'

'Everything, I regret to say. I don't consider myself to be as sharp as you, but the same explanation had occurred to me too. However, David explained that it couldn't have happened like that. For one thing, his grandmother enforced a strict rule that the overalls she provided could only be worn on her premises and Alice was forbidden even to take them home with her. That would be quite in character, of course, and I had no difficulty in believing it. Another objection is that, when David didn't hear from me on Saturday and was trying to make up his mind what to do, he took the handkerchief down to Alice's cottage, to ask if it belonged to her, but she denied it absolutely. She had no recollection of seeing it until it turned up on the ironing board. He was very tactful about it, mind you, pretended this was only an afterthought and that he'd really come to bring her week's wages, which he'd forgotten to leave out on Friday. That was the strict truth too, as it happens, all that side of life having been dealt with by his grandmother. I must say, Tessa, that he impressed me rather favourably yesterday. He's certainly leaning over backwards to do the right thing, without getting any of the neighbours into trouble, in the process. He spoke very kindly about Marc too.'

'Did he? What did he say about him?'

'Oh, just that he'd heard rumours that Marc had been involved in some stupid and unnecessary misunderstanding with the police, but that it had all been cleared up now and he knew what a tremendous relief that must be for me. I was really quite touched and I honestly believe that things are going to work out quite well in that quarter, specially if this girl he's going to marry turns out to be the right sort. Still, that does nothing to solve the immediate problem, does it? I still have to make some decision about that.'

'How long have you got?'

'I promised to try and ring him at lunch time and I really shouldn't keep him hanging about any longer than I can help, when he's been so considerate. Well, I'll just have to nerve myself to go and have a talk with Louise, I suppose,' Elsa said, getting up as she spoke. 'And the sooner the better, if it has to be done. I can't say I relish the prospect, but it seems the only one open to me. You'll be all right, will you? I shan't be long. At least, I hope not.'

'Yes, perfectly all right. I'll be sitting here, good as gold, keeping my fingers crossed for you, but . . .'

'And keep an eye on the children, will you? I don't want Marc to go vanishing into the blue again.'

'Okay, I'll do that too, but Elsa . . .'

'Well?' she asked, with a hint of impatience.

'This conversation you had with David yesterday, did it take place in the drawing room?'

'Well, yes, I suppose that's what you'd call it. Rather more like a doctor's waiting room than somewhere to sit and talk. Why do you want to know?'

'You didn't happen to notice a blown-up colour photograph, on a table near the window, or anywhere else in the room, for that matter?'

'No, I didn't.'

'You're sure of that?'

'Quite sure. It was the most dreary and impersonal room I've ever seen. I'd have noticed at once, if there'd been anything like that to catch the eye. But why do you want to know? What's the point of all this?'

'I don't really know,' I admitted, 'but I think I'll have to watch it. It shows signs of becoming an obsession.'

That was at nine o'clock and about half an hour later I uncrossed my fingers long enough to make some fresh toast and coffee for Marc, which he took upstairs on a tray, saying that he proposed to spend the morning working in his room.

I told him in all sincerity that I devoutly hoped he would not be disturbed.

He was followed into the kitchen shortly afterwards by Millie, at her most tousled and surly and, when she had masticated her way through a bowl of what looked like bran mash, I put it to her that she should wash her hair and I would set it for her in an entirely new style, which would enhance all her best features and probably cause Miss Diane Hearne to sit up and turn pale with rage.

She grudgingly consented to this and when the job was done I imprisoned her under my portable hair dryer, with instructions to remain there for a minimum of half an hour. It was then getting on for eleven o'clock, Elsa had still not returned and, with both my little charges safely occupied, the moment had come to uncross my fingers again and telephone Robin.

There was no good reason to suppose that he would have already dug out the information I had asked him to get for me, but it was worth a try, since the chance for a private talk might not come again for hours, perhaps days. The gamble paid off too, because he was gratifyingly informative, although, when I showered him with praise and thanks, he told me they were undeserved, since his success had been entirely gratuitous. It appeared that there had been a message on his desk that morning, requesting him to ring Inspector Bledlow as soon as he came in. Having done so and obliged with a little confidential, off-the-cuff information, whose nature he would not divulge, he was then in a position to ask a small favour in return.

'So tell me,' I said, 'and make it short and sharp, if you can. These walls may soon have ears. I take it she left a will?'

'Yes, indeed. Quite a recent one, in fact, dated about three months ago and a rather curious document, in some respects.'

'Doesn't he get the lot?'

'Not quite. That's to say he gets the house, the land and a reasonably hefty sum outright and with no conditions. He also stands to get half the residue, which I might tell you looks like coming out at well over the million mark, the other half going to some foundation in Australia.'

'What does "stands to get" mean?'

'There are strings to it. Very unusual ones too; something outside all my experience, at any rate. If he marries before his thirtieth birthday, this money goes into a trust for his heirs and he draws the income until they come of age.'

'And if not?'

'The foundation gets the lot.'

'And when is his thirtieth birthday?'

'Next February. So only four months to go.'

'Well, that shouldn't cause him any worry. He's unofficially engaged already and she's not half bad looking, if she's the girl in the photograph. I daresay they won't find it any harder to like each other when there's half a million or so depending on it.'

'Maybe not, but don't you find it an odd sort of clause?'

'Oh, I suppose that would be true, in a general way, but she was obviously a great old climber and she had set her heart on David taking things a step further by marrying into the aristocracy. Apart from the personal satisfaction, she would have seen it as one in the eye for all the people round here who she imagined had snubbed her.'

'Yes, but haven't you missed the point?'

'Oh, have I? Which point?'

'Well . . . if you don't see it, perhaps I've got it wrong. Legal terminology isn't exactly my forte . . .'

'And here comes Elsa, so I'd better go now. Goodbye, and thanks a lot, Robin.'

She was looking utterly spent and distraught and took the unprecedented step of flying to the gin bottle at ten past eleven in the morning.

'It was simply terrible,' she said, 'I came nearer to having a quarrel than I've been for years. And I never quarrel with anyone, Tessa,' she added, looking as though she might burst into tears if I disputed it.

150

'No, of course you don't, everyone knows that, so it must have been Louise's fault. Did she take it badly?'

'Badly is an understatement. It was most upsetting. I simply wouldn't have believed Louise could behave in such a way.'

'In such a what way?'

'Well, I was very careful to lead up to it tactfully, as you can imagine. The last thing I wanted was to shock or frighten her, but, when I eventually came out with it, her attitude at first was that I had meant to do precisely that. She practically accused me of having invented the story of the handkerchief out of pure malice. I could hardly believe my ears.'

'Did you manage to convince her that she was wrong?'

'In the end, I did, and a fat lot of good that was. When I asked her straight out whether she honestly believed me capable of such a mean, vicious and senseless trick, she mumbled something about not having meant that exactly, then launched out on a new tack and came up with a whole fresh set of accusations.'

'Quite a strong reaction, one way and another!'

'It was most unpleasant, I can assure you. The gist of it was that, all right, she was prepared to accept my word that I had not made the story up, but that could only mean that I was acting as the dupe or unintentional accomplice of someone else. In other words, instead of realising, as any true friend would have done, that the handkerchief had been planted in the Trelawney house, for the sole purpose of implicating Tim in the murder, I had been so perfidious as to swallow the story whole and believe the worst.'

'And what was your line of defence there?'

'I asked if she did not realise that what she was saying could only imply that someone actually had planted the handkerchief, perhaps for that very purpose, to which she calmly replied that she realised it perfectly.'

'I see!'

'I wonder if you do? I certainly didn't. My next question, naturally, was whether she had formed any idea of who that

151

person could be and that's when I really had to control myself not to punch her in the face.'

The picture conjured up by this statement was so improbable that I almost laughed aloud.

'There's nothing funny about it, my dear. She actually had the nerve to tell me that she quite frankly and firmly believed that the handkerchief had been put there by Marc. Can you credit it? I was so flabbergasted that at first I couldn't bring myself to utter a word and then she went on to say how, although she wouldn't dream of mentioning it to anyone else, she and I both knew he had been in the neighbourhood on the day of Mrs Trelawney's death. Hadn't we both seen and recognised his car? So what about that? Naturally, she wasn't accusing him of having had any hand in the murder, thanks very much, but, as far as she was concerned, there couldn't be any doubt that he was responsible for the handkerchief turning up where it did.'

'And when you could speak, what did you say?'

'Nothing much. I was having such a struggle not to lose my temper, you see. I simply told her that if that was how she felt, it might be better if she and I were not to meet for a while. I certainly had no wish to see her until she had apologised. Then I left her and came home and, as you see, had a strong drink to pull myself together.'

'Yes, very dignified and I consider you came out of it well, but how do you account for it, Elsa? What possessed her to make such an accusation, to you, of all people?'

For the first time her expression wavered and, turning her head away, she set the glass down on a table. Then she said slowly, 'I was asking myself the same question all the way home, until it suddenly came to me. Of course, the connection is entirely imaginery and it was still atrocious of her, but all at once I began to get a glimmer of what was in her mind.'

'Well, every little helps, I suppose?'

'It's all so stupid and miserable, but the fact is . . . well, do you remember my telling you the other day about Marc having this silly passion for practical jokes?'

'Yes, I do.'

'Well, some years ago, when he was about fifteen, I suppose, we all went to a New Year's Eve party at the Macadams. It was when their daughter was still alive. She was about the same age as Millie, so it was a kind of mixed-generations party and after dinner we played children's games, hide-and-seek and sardines and things like that.'

Elsa paused here, to pick up her drink again, while she drew on a seven-year-old memory. 'They had an au pair girl at the time, Norwegian or Swedish, I can't remember. Awfully pretty girl, but not very nice and Louise never really got on with her. Well, to be perfectly frank, we all thought she was a tiny bit jealous because Tim made such a ridiculous fuss of her and would insist on including her in all the family treats and outings. So, anyhow, that was the situation and during one of the games of sardines Marc was the first to go out of the room and he went and hid in this au pair's bedroom. Louise found him there. The bed was all rumpled up and he showed her one of Tim's handkerchiefs, which he said had been under the pillow. It was just for a lark and I'm sure he didn't understand in the least what he was doing. He was only a child, not . . . well, experienced, if you see what I mean, but it had the most fearful repercussions. Apparently, Tim and Louise had a blazing row after the party and two days later Karen was packed off home. That really scared poor Marc and he came to me and owned up. He'd messed up the bed himself and borrowed one of Tim's handkerchiefs, without telling him, in case it should come in handy for one of his silly pranks.'

'Did you tell Louise?'

'Certainly, I did. I made Marc come with me to see her there and then, to make a full confession and to apologise. She didn't take it very well and we were hardly on speaking terms for months afterwards. In a sad and curious way, it was really their child's death which brought us together again. Amazing to think that's already five or six years ago. It was such a dreadful time for them, you know; Tim, particularly.'

153

'Why particularly?'

'Because he was with her when it happened and, to some extent, I know he blamed himself. They were out on bicycles, going along in single file because the road was narrow and twisty. He was at the back and a car overtook him, travelling so fast that he only just had time to dismount. When he went round the next curve he saw that the child had been knocked off her bicycle and was lying in the road.'

'And the car hadn't stopped?'

'No, and he never got the number, or any proper sort of description. Naturally, his only concern at that moment was for his daughter.'

'Was she dead?'

'No, but she only survived for a few hours. That may have been just as well, in a sense, because there was serious brain damage, but you can imagine their agony. It does make me realise that I ought to be more tolerant when Louise has these funny moods.'

'It still doesn't give her the right to make those accusations against Marc.'

'No, it doesn't, but I suppose she'll pull herself together and come to her senses eventually. She must soon begin to realise that he wouldn't play a stupid trick like that at his age and also that the two events are entirely and utterly different.'

This may have been true, up to a point, yet nevertheless I could recognise certain similarities and one of them was Louise's violent and hostile reaction. It seemed to me that her anger on the first occasion could well have been provoked by the fact that she had found it all too easy to believe that Tim had been sleeping with the au pair girl. So could it not equally well have flared up now because, secretly, she found it just as easy to believe that he had been at Pettits Farm on the day of the murder?

'Thank you,' Toby said, when I telephoned him to turn in the latest report, 'I appreciate all the trouble you are going to on my behalf, but I am not sure it will do, you know. The hand-kerchief trick is a little banal, don't you agree? I seem to remember somebody using it before.'

'And I seem to remember someone else saying that life has a way of imitating art,' I remarked huffily.

'Yes, but this would be art imitating life, wouldn't it? Not quite the same thing and one has to draw the line some-where. In fact, if you want my honest opinion, I am not at all satisfied with the way things are working out. Perhaps it's time you went home and looked about for some plot ideas in London?'

'That might be all right from your point of view, Toby, but personally I do not consider that my work here is finished yet.'

'Oh, very well, suit yourself. And, of course, if anything at all original does turn up, I shall always be glad to hear about it,' he added graciously.

'I can't understand why you're staying on like this,' Robin complained when he rang that evening. After all, your excuse for going there in the first place was to protect a tree and prevent a murder and, without wishing to carp in any way, you can't claim to have been outstandingly successful in either. What is the use of prolonging it?'

'I feel I am being useful. Lending moral support and so on.'

'That's all very well, but how about me? No one needs moral support more than I do and I'm becoming absolutely sick to death of fish fingers. I really do think it's time you came home.'

'It's rather hard to put this without sounding rude and ungracious,' Elsa said after dinner, 'and that's the last thing I intend. It's been lovely having you here and no one could possibly be more grateful than I am for all your help and support. You've done wonders for Millie too, but I do realise that you have your own life to lead and it would be unfair to expect you to go on sacrificing yourself indefinitely. Well, what I'm trying to say is that I shall be sorry, but not in the least offended if you decide you want to go home tomorrow.'

That did it. If one of them had urged it on me, I might have listened. Two would doubtless have caused me to waver, but this three-pronged attack decided the matter.

'If it's all the same to you,' I said stiffly, 'and, providing it's not putting you to any inconvenience, I should like to stay until Friday.'

'But, of course, Tessa dear, I can't think of anything nicer. You are most welcome, you know that. Why Friday?' she asked, slightly tarnishing the gilt on the preceding remarks.

'Because that will give me three clear days to work on some facts I already possess and collect a few more which I still need.'

'What for?'

'To find out who killed Mrs Trelawney and why, and thereby to exonerate Marc publicly and permanently from any complicity whatsoever in her murder. Any objection?'

WEDNESDAY

Rarely can the unholy combination of injured pride, defiance and bravado have caused a neck to stick out more dangerously and it did not take long to grasp that some fast thinking would be required, if I were not to get my head chopped off on the coming Friday. More discouraging still was the dawning realisation that thinking would not be enough. I had already developed a theory concerning the motive for the murder and thus of the murderer's identity, and when I had listed all the known facts which had contributed to this conclusion, I could not find one which contained a flaw. Unfortunately, I could not find one which offered proof either and I knew that, were I to present Inspector Bledlow with every scrap of information I had gathered, which had been my original intention, whether he agreed with me or not, he still would not have nearly enough evidence to make an arrest.

There was only one way out that I could see and that was to force or provoke the murderer into some spontaneous indiscretion, whereby he would betray himself beyond the point of retreat, and, after everyone had gone to bed on Monday night, I lay awake for several hours, wondering how this was to be done.

Sleeplessness produced no positive results whatever and all I got for my pains was a slight headache and a tendency to yawn my way through breakfast on Tuesday morning. A stroll in the fresh air, followed by a period of meditation on the ridge overlooking the sad remains of the oak tree proved equally fruitless and by Tuesday evening only Elsa's compassionate, faintly amused expression whenever she glanced my way stopped me from caving in and admitting defeat.

By Wednesday morning I had made up my mind that there was nothing for it but to take action, since any action, however ill-conceived, must be preferable to mooning about and waiting for something to happen. So, as soon as Elsa had left for the Parish Hall, to discuss plans and preparations for the Harvest Supper, I set forth to put myself in the lion's den and see what reaction I got, the den in this case being a ramshackle old barn which had been converted into a pottery.

There was always the chance, of course, that the lion would not be at home, or, equally frustrating, that there would be a cub or two around as well, but I considered myself reasonably safe from both these hazards. Marigold's inquest, with its highly predictable verdict, had taken place on the previous day and the local schools had now reopened for the Autumn term. So it was difficult to see how even Diane could justify further absenteeism. Whereas, faced with this gaping emptiness, both figurative and real, I guessed that James Hearne's instinct, if he were typical of craftsmen in general, would prompt him to seek solace in a stint of hard work.

Also to be taken into account was the risk of being recognised, but I did not take this very seriously either. Nothing I had heard about them indicated that any of the Hearne family took a lively interest in the performing arts and I also knew that they did not possess a television set. I had picked up this item from Millie, who, in a particularly caustic mood, had told me that one of the things that had put such a strain on Marc's relationship with Diane had been her extreme reluctance to go for moonlight drives, or listen to records in his room, preferring to sit hand in hand with him on the drawing room sofa, watching television; this, as she frequently explained, being such a rare treat for her.

A green, slightly sagging fence surrounded the small front garden and on either side of the gate was a small notice board, with stencilled lettering and pinioned to the ground by a wooden peg. The one on the right said *Orchard House* and the other, which also had a left pointing arrow painted on it, *Sowerley Potteries.*

I pushed the gate open, which was not easy to do, since it had come half way off its hinges and had to be held up with both hands to prevent it scraping along the ground, walked up the path, lifted the tongue shaped iron knocker and beat a tattoo on the front door.

To my relief, three or four minutes went by without any kind of response and, having eliminated the first hazard, I walked round to the back of the house, peering through windows into deserted rooms as I passed.

The garden here was much larger and open on all sides, but set in such sharply downward sloping land that it was not altogether surprising that no one had recently shown much enthusiasm for mowing the grass. There was an empty, scrubby looking meadow to the right of this erstwhile lawn, with the orchard over on the other side, and, standing with my back to the house, I could see right down into the hollow and up again to Geoffrey's cottage on the far side, and thus was able to verify a point which had been bothering me ever since the night time assault on the oak tree.

Beyond the gnarled, neglected looking apple and pear trees on my left I could see what I took to be the barn which housed the pottery works but, not being greatly attracted to the idea of approaching it by way of the orchard, I went round to the front of the house again and through a side gate in the fence until I came to the muddy yard surrounding the barn. This was empty, except for an ancient looking kiln and a huge mound of broken and rejected pottery.

There was no one in sight, but a light was on inside the barn and I could hear a man's voice, which was bad news, unless Mr Hearne made a habit of talking to himself. I had no reason to suppose he did not, but nevertheless felt tempted, at this point, to content myself with the one new fact, or rather confirmation of a fact which I had already gleaned, and slink away to the car. However, before I had quite succumbed, a man appeared in the open doorway, which was straight ahead of me, at a distance of about twenty yards.

'Ha!' he announced in ringing tones. 'So my senses did not deceive me! I felt a presence hovering just beyond my orbit and lo! You are looking for someone!'

For some reason, which I found hard to pin down, everything I had heard about James Hearne had conspired to create a picture in my imagination of a small, ineffectual and unassertive man, probably with a wispy, unkempt beard and pale, watery eyes. Now that the real one had stood up, I realised that the only part of this identikit which still applied was the beard and this, too, was much more shaggy and bold looking than I had visualised it.

He was a tall, once good-looking man, broad shouldered and with powerful hands and piercing, slightly demented blue eyes. He was dressed like a labourer and his face was criss-crossed with deeply grooved lines, which looked as though they had been etched in with pen and ink, although, judging by his finger nails, this too could have been merely honest grime.

'You are looking for someone!' he said again. 'You need help!'

They were statements, not questions, and I understood instantly that he did not suppose me to have lost my way and to be in need of directions, but that the help I sought sprang from some anguish of the soul and, unable to resist the histrionic impulse to respond in kind, I took two steps forward.

'Yes! Yes . . .' I said, then dried completely, for it had been a most treacherous impulse.

During the preceding year or two I must have read not less than half a dozen novels and seen as many movies in which at least one character was crying out for help, in some form or other, but the ludicrous thing was that I was now quite unable to recall a single example of what they had needed it for. The only feeble idea that came to mind was to tell him that I wanted to find myself, but as this was quite untrue I doubted if I could put much conviction into it and stood gaping at him, like a fish whose only requirement was help

160

in getting off the hook. He was probably used to it though, because it did not bother him in the least and he came up close, put an arm round my shoulders, which was really quite unpleasant, and propelled me towards the barn.

Despite the door and windows being wide open, the interior was dank and dusty and so chaotically untidy that it was hard to see how anything of value could be constructed there. However, when he took me on a guided tour, explaining the various processes of his work and finally into the section where the painting was done, I realised that he was not only a prolific, but also a highly talented craftsman.

'Thank you,' he said, when I had expressed my admiration. 'You have a discerning eye, which is as I had expected. So now you know everything that is important about me, and how about you? What is perplexing you and what did you want to ask me?'

He seemed a harmless enough man, despite his odd manner and farouche appearance and I have a weakness for artists who make things with their hands, so I took a chance and said, 'I suppose I really wanted to ask you about a murder.'

He was not fazed for a second and answered as readily as though we had been discussing a cricket match, 'Yes, I rather thought so, and that is a pity.'

'Why?'

'Because it is one of the few subjects on which I can be of no help to you. I consider such judgements are best left to God and I advise you to seek help from Him.'

I knew then that I was wasting my time. He was either putting on a marvellous act, or else was quite as dotty as first appearances had suggested. Either way, there was never any blood to be got out of this stone and the only consolation was that, if he had said nothing to confirm my theory, he had certainly said nothing to refute it either.

I had started to thank him for his advice and to say goodbye, when he put a finger to his mouth, enjoining me to be silent. 'Hush! Another presence has come amongst us! I can sense it!'

We were standing right over at the far end of the barn by then and I could neither see, hear, nor sense anything of this new presence, but he went striding over towards the door, full of glad confidence. I followed more slowly, not being so accustomed to picking my way through the layers of rubble which littered the floor. When I joined him he was standing squarely in the doorway, gazing out at an empty void.

'Gone before I could reach out to it,' he announced.

'Or perhaps you were mistaken?'

'No I am never mistaken. She was here and she has gone.'

'She? How do you know it was a she, if you never saw it?'

'Quite simple; it was a female presence. My daughter, as it happens,' he added, in a matter of fact voice.

'Your daughter?' I repeated nervously.

'My eldest daughter. She should be at her work today, but she wanted to stay at home and look after me. Quite unnecessary, of course, I am more than capable of attending to my few meagre wants, but the truth is that we've had a great sorrow in our family, and I believe the poor child feels unequal to facing her employers and colleagues just at present.'

'But you are sure she was here?'

'Quite sure. She has a very strong aura, like yours. I always know when she is close at hand.'

I believed him and I did not know whether to feel sorry, or glad, or merely slightly uneasy.

I had expected them to act fast and, for practical purposes, this suited me well, my deadline being then only twenty-four hours away, but I had seriously underestimated both their ingenuity and the degree of desperation to which their actions had brought them and, as a result, was very nearly caught, quite literally, on the wrong foot. Also, although it was all over months ago now, I still occasionally have waking nightmares, remembering how close this state of unpreparedness brought Marc and Millie to the edge of danger as well.

On Wednesday afternoon, while still unsure how far my cat had got in among the pigeons, I had suggested to Marc, who had already shown signs of possessing a strong nostalgic streak, that it might be fun for the three of us to take a picnic to our old haunt, up on the ridge at the edge of the woods, as we had done so often in our carefree youth.

He and Millie had been all in favour of the plan and Elsa had also thrown herself into it with great verve, concocting a picnic tea of hard boiled eggs, marmite sandwiches and plum cake, which had been the regular fare on those earlier occasions.

Unfortunately, however, the cart had gone before the horse this time, in that our destination had been chosen for its own sake and not, as previously, because the afternoon was so hot and airless as to make the cool breeze blowing across our hilltop seem particularly inviting. On that Wednesday afternoon the breeze which whistled through the garden was sharp enough to be unpleasant and up on the ridge it had stiffened to something approaching gale force.

'This won't do,' Millie said gloomily. 'We'd better go back into the woods a little way.'

Afterwards I wished we had taken her advice, but Marc's passion for tradition went deeper than I had bargained for and he rounded on her contemptuously. 'Don't be such a pathetic, silly clot! How can we go back into the woods when all we'll see there are a lot of trees? What about our view? Don't you remember that the view was the whole point?'

I let them fight it out between themselves, which was quite a treat for them, and it ended in an amicable compromise. By keeping to the edge of the wood for another fifty yard or so and then dropping down about twice that distance towards the hollow, we had our backs to the wind, shelter all around and almost, although not quite, the old authentic view. The difference was that instead of having a sideways view of Geoffrey's cottage, we were now looking up towards it and it was partially hidden by what remained of the oak tree.

There was to be another upset in our normal placid programme too, and this one was far more serious. It did not occur until we were half way through our picnic and the first intimation came from the unmistakable sound of a tractor engine coming from somewhere above and behind us. Swivelling round, we saw that there was not only a tractor, but that it had a trailer of some kind attached to it, somewhat resembling a huge iron bedstead, with spikes underneath. It had obviously come from one of the new barns and, on reaching the narrow, flat strip of ground at the top of the field, it turned away at right angles and moved slowly off in the direction of Orchard House and the Macadams.

Marc and Millie applied themselves to their boiled eggs and sandwiches once more, but some sixth sense, which I was forever afterwards so grateful to know I possessed, impelled me to keep watching.

'Any more tea in that thermos?' Millie asked, but I ignored her because it seemed to me that the tractor driver had now either changed his mind, or more likely, seeing how precariously he had positioned himself, had lost control of the steering. The trailer was still horizontal, but the front wheels of the tractor had made a half turn and had started to dip downwards.

Totally fascinated, I continued to watch, as the wheels continued to turn and descend. Then, with a huge lurch, the trailer also started to twist sideways, the whole contraption gathered speed and I realised in a blinding flash what was about to happen.

Springing up, I shouted, 'On your feet, both of you! And start running! Don't turn round and don't stop! Just keep running!'

There was nothing wrong with their reflexes and, struggling against the wind, we reached the edge of the wood, panting for breath, in a dead heat. It was none too soon either, because when we did turn and look down there were two wide grey parallel strips along the rug, where the wheels had passed over it, with the picnic basket, curiously enough, quite untouched and sitting sedately between them.

The tractor was by this time genuinely out of control, careering faster every second as the slope grew steeper and heading straight for the oak tree, which stood inexorably in its path, like some proud and battered Nemesis. We waited in horror and fascination for the inevitable and fatal collision.

'He's mad!' Millie muttered. 'Did you see his face? I did look round for a second, although you said not to, and he was coming at us like that on purpose.'

'I know. An uncontrollable impulse, I imagine.'

'Utterly, raving mad!' she repeated.

'As you were the first to point out,' I reminded her.

THURSDAY

'It was the handkerchief that clinched it,' I told my assembled audience. 'You said it was too old a trick, Toby, and you were right. In this case, it was also a very misguided one, although fairly typical of that snapper up of unconsidered trifles, who probably pinched the idea from the incident all those years ago at the New Year's Eve party.'

'Do you mean he planted it himself?' Elsa asked.

'Oh yes, but only after their plans had gone wrong and they were getting desperate. It didn't figure in the original script and therefore was too hastily conceived and carried out. I mean, just think of it! How could one of Tim's handkerchiefs have found its way into the Trelawneys' washing machine by accident? One theory was that the police had overlooked it because, by the time they arrived on the scene, it had already gone into the kitchen laundry bin, but that's not very plausible, is it? One can hardly imagine Tim putting it there himself and, when David came back that evening and discovered his grandmother's corpse, he would presumably have had other things on his mind than tidying away stray handkerchiefs.'

Marc had now returned to London, swapping over with Robin, who, giving as his reason that he could not rely on me to keep my promise to release him from the bondage of fish fingers until he had personally seen me off the premises, was spending the night at the Grange, and who now said, 'I suppose your reference to their plans having gone wrong implied that, much to their fury and disappointment, Marc was not already in custody and awaiting trial?'

'Oh, don't!' Elsa begged. 'It still makes me shudder to think that anyone could be so wicked.'

'I'm afraid it's true, all the same,' I told her. 'You see, they obviously realised that their carefully laid plan to make it look like an ordinary break-in, which for some reason had gone wrong and turned violent, might not hold up and that if the police should be bright enough to see through it, then negative evidence alone would not be enough to keep them out of trouble and they would need a scapegoat. He had all the opportunity that anyone could need, but no apparent motive; whereas Diane had a perfectly genuine alibi, that trip to Bexhill having been timed to coincide with the Darby and Joan tea party and the rehearsal for Millie's protest march. That left a clear field for him to come here and borrow Març's car for a couple of hours. The object of that, need I tell you, being to ensure that Alice would get a clear view of it when she left at four o'clock and later give a description to the police? So that left poor old Marc, ostensibly with the perfect opportunity, plus a motive which he had been loudly trumpeting around for months past to all and sundry. They must really have believed that, between them, they had contrived a trap which could never be sprung.'

'You know what, though?' Millie said. 'Marc didn't really have much of a motive, in fact hardly any at all, once Diane had broken off her engagement and he no longer had to play Sir Galahad. I wonder what made her do it?'

'Well, personally, I'm glad she did,' Elsa informed us. 'You'll say I'm silly, I expect, but I like to think she had one redeeming feature and at least she had the decency to end her engagement to one young man, when she'd made up her mind to marry another.'

Toby raised his head and addressed the ceiling. 'I feel I may be forced to drop Elsa. Audiences would never believe that anyone could be so trusting.'

'And Millie shows signs of taking aiter her,' I remarked.

'What are they both talking about, please, Robin?'

'Oh, I'll let Tessa explain. It's her evening, after all.'

'Tessa?'

'Well, don't you see, both of you, that Marc didn't know it had been broken off until two days after the murder had been committed? That was why poor little Diane became so agitated, Millie, when you tried to persuade her to ring him up on this telephone. That was the last thing she wanted, but on the other hand she wouldn't have dared give him the push once he'd been arrested. That would have made some bad dents in the sweet, loyal little image she wanted the world to believe in. Moreover, she might have been stuck in that situation for God knows how long and she and David only had a few months left, if they were to collect that extra half million. Therefore, it was essential for her to break things off, technically, with Marc before the murder, but to make sure that it only became effective, as it were, after-wards. One has to say that she played it rather cunningly, but in no way was she trying to do Marc a good turn. In fact, in my opinion, the only one you owe any gratitude to is Mrs Trelawney.'

'What have I to thank her for, for heaven's sake?'

'For coming to live here and introducing her grandson into your midst. Diane had started getting her dainty claws on Marc when she was about twelve years old, recognising as far back as that that he was easily the most eligible and attractive boy likely to come her way, and nothing in this world was going to alter that, until Baby Face turned up, with all that vast fortune in the offing.'

'Yes, I suppose it's true, but I'm still rather puzzled about that. We had all been given to understand that he was about to marry someone quite different, such a grand and splendid girl, indeed, that we felt we might all be expected to curtsey to her. Did she never exist? Was she just another invention to put everyone off the scent?'

'Oh no, she existed all right, at least in the beginning. He really was on the brink of becoming formally engaged to someone of that description in the early days. There was a photograph to prove it and it was one reason why his grand-mother was so enchanted with him and so eager to indulge his every whim. But then one day he went to inspect Orchard House, which had been earmarked for him and his bride, and there he met Diane, which changed everything. Even if he wasn't instantly bowled over, and I daresay he was, it wouldn't have taken her a couple of seconds to see that this was where her really big chance lay and she'd have gone after it with all the wiles she possessed. Everything else followed from that, because they knew from the outset that Mrs Trelawney would never have left him all her money if he'd dashed her hopes by running off with this nonentity of a girl, from such a humble, not to mention unstable background, and he certainly wouldn't have been quite so attractive to Diane without the money. So, from their point of view, there was only one way out and they took it.'

Robin said. 'I always considered that clause in her will to have been carelessly worded and you must agree that this bears me out?'

'Yes, it does; but I suppose that's the price she paid for being so arrogant and for believing herself to be cleverer than anyone else. And I think the explanation must be that she had begun to realise that David's official romance was cooling off, though never for one moment suspecting that it was on account of a rival attraction just up the road. He and Diane were much too canny for that. She probably thought it was the girl in the jodhpurs who was beginning to lose interest, so she decided to make an offer, first verbally and then written into her will, which neither of them could refuse. I daresay it would have been in her nature to assume that this was the surest way of bringing the young couple to heel.'

'So that explains why the second photograph disappeared,' Millie said. 'I can see that he'd have wanted all the records and rumours about his first love to be wiped out and forgotten as quickly as possible, once his grandmother was dead; but what about the other one, the one of Geoffrey's tree?'

'Ah well, you see, Millie, the tree really had nothing much to do with it. You and I happened to be concentrating on it and so we didn't pay any attention at all to what was going on elsewhere. I can't ever prove this, naturally, but it's my

169

belief that in one of our shots we'd quite inadvertently included something which could have seriously damaged their carefully preserved pretence of being virtual strangers, if not declared enemies. If you remember, when we first caught sight of her, Diane was just beginning her climb down the slope towards the tree and she was quite alone. But just supposing that only a minute or two earlier she and David had been standing together and talking to each other like the love birds they were? With Geoffrey no longer around to observe them, they might easily have allowed the mask to slip, if they'd happened to meet by chance. And do you also remember what a spin she went into when she looked up and saw us leaning on the fence and brandishing our camera? She tried to make out that she was nervous that we'd disapprove of her using Geoffrey's garden as a short cut. As though he'd have cared! My theory is that she had realised in a flash that, whether we had consciously witnessed it or not, something of that damning little scene between her and David might actually have been recorded on photograph. Isn't that the only logical explanation for her first pinching the camera and then, having found what she feared to find, destroying one of the prints?'

Toby said. 'I know how it bolsters your ego when we all keep asking questions and, besides, I have a professional interest at stake, so tell me this: was that little episode really enough to suggest to you that there might be something going on between those two? If so, even I must congratulate you!'

'Well, don't kill yourself over it, because there'd been an earlier one still, which seemed to involve a cover-up of some kind, and with Diane again in the thick of it. It was when the oak tree was attacked in the light of headlamps. Louise had noticed them the instant she got home from searching for her dog, and yet no one at Orchard House appeared to have done so. Or if they had, they'd paid not the slightest attention. Naturally, my curiosity only concerned three people. The younger children were probably in bed and asleep at the time and I eliminated Mrs Hearne for even more obvious reasons. But that still left Diane and Marigold and their father, and Diane, in particular, always made such a great fuss about being so attached to Geoffrey. That was partly why I made my expedition to the Pottery yesterday. I wanted to make sure that they really did have a clear view of the tree from their back windows. Well, of course, I felt I was already getting towards the explanation of why Diane might have seen it plainly and still taken no action and why she might have prevented Marigold from taking any, but there was still Dad to consider. I was keen to find out whether he was batty enough to commit murder, to save himself the trouble of moving house.'

'And, personally, I'm rather sorry you failed,' Toby said. 'He was always my number one fancy. I rather liked the idea of his persuading himself that he was acting as the instrument of God, or something on those lines.'

'Even so, the mission couldn't exactly go down in history as a failure, because when I discovered that Diane had been secretly snooping around and no doubt listening to every word, I felt sure I was on the right track. I guessed that she'd warn David that I was moving in too close and I thought it was just a question of sitting back and waiting for one of them to do something desperate. Unfortunately, I didn't expect it to happen quite so soon, or to be quite so desperate; but then, as Millie once pointed out, he really was mad. He and Diane were made for each other.'

'And, in a sense, he died for love of her,' Toby reminded us. 'She has that consolation. Not to mention getting off scot free, herself, which may give cause for even greater satisfaction.'

Elsa said, 'And, as far as I'm concerned, it leaves only one more question to be answered. It's about the car keys. I understand now who removed the spare set and why, but who put them back? Not David, as we know, and surely not Diane either? She would hardly have dared walk in the house and calmly put them away in my drawer, when she

171

had just treated Marc so abominably and ran the risk of coming face to face with him?'

'No, this is where Marigold enters the picture,' I explained. 'I think that's what she was on her way to do when Millie met her in the lane last Saturday afternoon, just a few hours before she killed herself. Do you remember, Millie? You said she was in a state about something and also that she could only have been on her way here.'

'Oh, for God's sake, don't remind me, Tessa! I still feel awful about it.'

'Well, you needn't, because I'd just dealt her a far crueller blow myself; only that too was unintentional.'

'Now how can that be?' Robin asked. 'I understood you'd never actually seen Marigold? Besides, if memory serves, we'd spent practically the whole of that afternoon on the telephone, trying to find Marc.'

'Yes, so we did and one of the people I spoke to was Marigold. I pretended to be calling from the Pettits estate office and I told her that David Trelawney wanted to get in touch with Diane. She was absolutely dazed and appalled and she must have felt she was really going right out of her mind, poor girl. She had the best of all reasons, after all, for believing that David knew exactly where Diane was and exactly when she'd be back.'

'But you told us that they managed to keep their relationship a secret from everyone?'

'No, I didn't say everyone; although I'm sure they made very, very few exceptions. On the other hand, it wouldn't altogether surprise me if James Hearne had picked up some vibrations about how the land lay, which was probably what made him so cheerful and optimistic about everything coming up roses in the end. And Marigold must have been let into the secret too, at some point, don't you agree? How else can one account for her bearing up so well during the period when the family was living under the threat of eviction and then going completely to pieces when Mrs Trelawney was murdered and, on the face of it, things were

172

about to take a turn for the better?'

'You mean Marigold knew who the murderer was?'

'I'm afraid she must have guessed. That was the strain she was living under, which finally became too much for her; and that was why she addressed her suicide note to Diane, saying that she knew Diane would understand and forgive her. I suppose what happened was that in the first triumphant flush of her splendid new romance, Diane confided in Marigold, swearing her to secrecy, of course, and then later on, when they needed an ally, to pass on telephone messages and so on, Marigold, being easily the most sane and sensible one available, was the obvious choice. Unfortunately, she was rather too sane and sensible for her own good.'

'Yes, it's dreadfully sad,' Elsa sighed, 'and it removes my very last shred of pity for that wicked, detestable girl. Well, my dear, you have explained it all beautifully and I do congratulate you. You have been so amazingly thorough and I'm sure Inspector Bledlow should be grateful to you.'

'I'm not, though,' Toby informed her. 'She has been much too thorough for my liking. It seems to me that the only thing she has left for anyone else to do is to write the damn thing.'